S0-ACY-491

Heat.

It scorched through her. His lips were gentle and seeking and in that first surprised instant she forgot to pull back, forgot to analyze. Instead, she gave herself to the kiss, let herself experience it, the touch of his lips to hers an intimate joining.

She pulled back and recognized the sound of a cheer from the crowd. What on earth had she just done?

Logan's gaze sought hers. Something serious in those dark eyes quickly transformed into amusement.

He winked. "Not so icy after all, princess."

Dear Reader,

I have to confess to a soft spot for self-made men. It's one of the reasons I've so enjoyed writing *Falling for the Princess*. Logan Buchanan has made his way in the world by setting goals and implementing strategies for achieving them. And at the start of this book he has a plan. He thinks it's a good plan, a great plan. It'll get him precisely what he wants.

But a man shouldn't get everything he wants—it's not good for him. Which is where Rebecca Marconi comes in, a woman unlike anyone Logan has met before. Unbeknownst to either of them she's about to show him the difference between what he thinks he wants and what he actually needs.

I also wanted to say a special thank you to those of you who contacted me after I first wrote about the Marconi family to ask for Rebecca's story. Here it is.

Happy reading,

Sandra

SANDRA HYATT

FALLING FOR
THE PRINCESS

Recycling programs
for this product may
not exist in your area.

ISBN-13: 978-0-373-73113-8

FALLING FOR THE PRINCESS

www.Harlequin.com

Printed in U.S.A.

Books by Sandra Hyatt

Silhouette Desire

Having the Billionaire's Baby #1956
The Magnate's Pregnancy Proposal #1991
His Bride for the Taking #2022
Under the Millionaire's Mistletoe #2056
  "Mistletoe Magic"
Revealed: His Secret Child #2072

Harlequin Desire

Falling for the Princess #2100

SANDRA HYATT

After completing a business degree, traveling and then settling into a career in marketing, Sandra Hyatt was relieved to experience one of life's eureka! moments while on maternity leave—she discovered that writing books, although a lot slower, was just as much fun as reading them.

She knows life doesn't always hand out happy endings and figures that's why books ought to. She loves being along for the journey with her characters as they work around, over and through the obstacles standing in their way.

Sandra has lived in both the U.S. and England and currently lives near the coast in New Zealand with her high school sweetheart and their two children.

You can visit her at www.sandrahyatt.com.

To Mum and Dad

One

"You're going about this all wrong." The deep, low voice shattered the serenity of the bright fall morning.

It sounded like...

But it couldn't be. Not here.

Regardless of the impossibility, Rebecca Marconi's fingers tightened around the handle of her mug and she looked warily over her shoulder. The dark-haired man at the beachfront café's only other occupied table lowered his newspaper and raised his sunglasses.

Amusement glinted in Logan Buchanan's chocolate-colored eyes.

The last person she expected to see. The last person she *wanted* to see. Rebecca shook her head, disbelieving. "Where do I have to go to get away from you?"

"To the ends of the earth, Princess."

"I thought I had." She'd spent the past two weeks traveling across Europe and North America until, after a twelve-hour flight and a drive a third of that time, she'd ended up on a remote part of a remote peninsula in New Zealand. Here, along the whole sweep of beach before her, she could see fewer than half a dozen people.

Of all the cafés in all the towns in all the world... "How did you find me?"

Straight dark eyebrows lifted. "Please. Give me some credit. You haven't exactly been discreet."

Actually, she'd tried. She'd attended just two unavoidable gatherings of friends, one in New York, and one in San Francisco. She hadn't expected either of those gatherings to end up on celebrity gossip websites. Her friends weren't the type to court publicity. She couldn't, however, say the same for the friends of her friends. That was the trouble, you never really knew who else was at these things or what they truly wanted no matter how innocent and open they seemed. It was a lesson she ought to have learned before now. "Sophie's engagement party?"

"To name but one."

Here, finally, she'd been planning on laying low for a time while she figured out a way forward. A way that would work for both her and her father, the reigning monarch of the small European principality of San Philippe.

She wasn't well-known outside of Europe—outside of San Philippe even. Here, she'd counted on some privacy and anonymity. "I was going to go home." She left the *eventually* off of her sentence.

She'd turned down the two unexpected requests from Logan to meet with him in the week before she left home. She'd been busy, but she'd also seen no reason to meet with a man who'd made his views on royalty and the archaic ways of her country abundantly clear.

A man who also always managed to unsettle her, making her feel as though she didn't quite fit her own skin.

"I don't have that much time," he said.

"I have a news flash for you, Logan. This isn't about you. It's about me."

"It always is."

She met his steady gaze, kept her own unflinching. There were times when her training—to show no reaction—came in handy. "That was unkind. Even for you." She wouldn't let herself care what he thought.

He'd arrived in San Philippe a few months ago, introduced into society by her brother Rafe. And he'd been an immediate hit with both the men and the women. The women, for his looks and for the down-to-earth honesty and Chicago charm that was, admittedly, a refreshing change from the restrained niceties of royal circles; and the men, for his phenomenal business success and skill on the polo field that had helped their team to its last three wins.

For a time she, too, had been secretly captivated. There was something so different about him.

Rebecca turned back to her hot chocolate. That time had passed. She'd *made* it pass.

She felt a movement beside her and watched from the corner of her eye as he stood. If he left, even for a short while, she could head back to her bed-and-breakfast, collect her bags and leave. And this time she would be even more discreet. He wasn't the only thing she'd been trying to escape in San Philippe so it hadn't occurred to her that he'd follow her. But now that she knew…

Dashing her hopes, Logan set his espresso on her table, pulled out the chair beside her and lowered himself into it, seeming almost too big—too broad-shouldered and long-limbed for the ornate wrought-iron chair. As he stretched out his denim-clad legs his foot brushed against hers.

Rebecca tucked her feet beneath her chair and picked up her mug, cradling it with both hands as though it could provide some kind of shield. What would it be like to say what was on her mind, to meet his unspoken challenges head-on? To leave her feet where they were, touching his? To return that direct gaze, not backing down? She wouldn't—couldn't—know. Even here she was still who she was. A member of a royal family. And that position dictated her actions and words every waking minute.

Her thoughts and her dreams were another matter. Fortunately, nobody could see inside her head. Unfortunately, not even she could always control the direction of those thoughts and dreams.

For now, all she wanted was for Logan to leave her be. "I don't suppose asking you to go away is going to work?"

"No. But you could try ordering me to go away. Make it a royal command. I dare you." Challenge glinted in his eyes.

And wouldn't he just love that, the opportunity to laugh at someone trying to order him to do anything. "I know what you think of royalty and of me." His honesty hadn't been quite so refreshing when it was directed at her. She must have met other people who shared his thoughts on royalty—she just didn't know who they were because they hid their sentiments from her. She'd tried to be glad of Logan's honesty. But his openly voiced opinions had had her questioning herself, her role in her country, her future. "So, why have you followed me here?"

"I had business here. Meeting you is a happy coincidence, given your inability to see me in San Philippe."

"I'm sure you don't believe in coincidence any more

than I do. And I don't believe for a moment that you have business here."

"No? But coincidences happen all the time and I have interests all over the world."

"America and Europe, yes. But not here."

The light in his eyes changed. "I didn't realize you paid such attention to my activities."

"I don't." She felt as if she'd stepped into a verbal trap. "I listen when people talk, that's all. It would be rude not to."

"Of course." Amusement glimmered.

It was that easy for him to undermine her. A fact he seemed to be infuriatingly aware of. "Don't pretend to agree with me when you don't. The very least I've come to expect from you is honesty. Usually brutal."

"Now who's being unkind?"

"I'm sorry. Did I injure your delicate feelings?"

He threw back his head and laughed and she couldn't remember whether she'd ever heard that sound from him. She decided on not. Because surely she wouldn't have forgotten the rich warm depths that seemed so at odds with the self-serving businessman. The sound—and the mirth behind it—coaxed an involuntary smile in return. And for a moment their shared amusement created a tenuous bond that warmed her. Made her feel not quite so alone.

She quelled the smile. She had to. He'd see it as a weakness. And she'd once heard him attribute his success in business and in sport to discerning his opponents' weaknesses and exploiting them. "Just tell me what you want, Logan. I'll try to help."

He met and held her gaze. "I want you."

The three baldly spoken words hung in the air and any desire to smile evaporated. Rebecca swallowed. For just a moment she imagined the possible interpretations. No man had ever said those words to her and she would have much preferred not to have heard them from this man and in this particular circumstance. Would a man like him, raw and honest, ever want someone like her, whose existence was founded on birthright and image?

She ought not to care.

"What do you really want?" She tried for a look of royal disdain, but the only result was a broadening of his smile, effectively conveying just how little her so-called disdain meant to him.

"I've told you."

"That you want me? No. You might want what I can do for you. But you don't want me." She knew how things worked. She held political sway in San Philippe.

"And if I did want you?" He imbued the words with a hint of curiosity. Again, possible interpretations flickered in her imagination.

She had to end this now. The words, the low tone, the possibilities his question raised—and her resulting foolishness—almost hurt. "Stop wasting my time, Logan."

"Time you're clearly using so productively." He glanced at her hot chocolate and the cuisine magazine on the table beside it.

Contrary to what he thought, she didn't get to spend a lot of time doing nothing in particular. She treasured it when she did. Rebecca stood. "If you're not going to go away, then I will." Leaving the magazine and the drink she'd had only a few sips of, she walked back along the beach. She headed for the rocky promontory at the end of the bay, the Pacific Ocean on one side of her, a quiet strip of luxury housing on the other. And behind the houses a steep, forested hillside.

He took so long to catch up with her she'd almost allowed herself to believe it would be that easy. But his shadow, long from the setting sun, came into view, drawing level with hers. As he fell into step beside her, he handed her a take-out cup. "You hardly touched your drink."

"Thank you." What else could she say?

"Hot chocolate? I'd have thought you were more a cappuccino kind of girl."

"Coffee keeps me awake if I drink it at this time of day."

"You have trouble sleeping?"

She hadn't meant to give him anything so personal. "Logan, I'm hardly going to discuss my sleeping habits with you. In fact, I'm not going to discuss anything with you. So you may as well go."

"Order me to."

She had nothing to lose by trying. She took a deep breath. "I command you, in the name of my father, to go away."

Rebecca managed to get several paces ahead of him while he was doubled over with laughter, and she couldn't quite help her own smile at the futility of her attempt. She'd never actually tried issuing a royal command before. Now she knew why.

He jogged to catch up. "But your father, and what he wants you to do, is the reason I'm here."

Any desire to smile faded. She'd feared as much, ever since Logan's first request to meet with her. The timing, so soon after her father's announcement, had been too coincidental to be anything else. "I'm dealing with it. In my own way."

"Which is where we come back to what I said at the outset. You're going about this all wrong. But I have an idea that might help."

"I'm not going to ask. I have no desire to hear your thoughts on my private life." Though her private life—thanks to her father—was rapidly becoming even more public than usual. They walked past the gated entrance to her bed-and-breakfast, which was tucked up in the forested hillside. She didn't so much as look at the steep-roofed building and its inviting balcony. It was quiet and quaint and not at all the style of place she usually vacationed. But it had been cleared by security for her to stay at. One of her brothers had even stayed here a year ago. Logan wouldn't know that and it certainly wouldn't be where the high-flying businessman would expect to find her.

"You don't want my advice?" he asked, friendly and helpful.

"I'll bet the wolf sounded just like you when he told Little Red Riding Hood about the shortcut through the woods." She glanced at him. "And the smile was probably similar, too." That smile broadened. Red Riding Hood, naive and innocent, wouldn't have stood a chance against the tempting warmth so silkily offered.

They walked on, sun shining on their backs, the surf rolling in beside them—it could almost have been pleasant. The sort of quiet stroll along the beach she'd dreamed of. Except in her dreams there was a man at her side who wanted her, not something *from* her. Fifteen minutes later they reached the end of the bay. A track led into the forest, a weathered sign announced a steep twenty-minute walk to the lookout point. Rebecca started up the track and Logan followed. Despite the shade, sweat was trickling down her back and between her breasts by the time she reached the top. Below and beyond, the white-edged bay swept toward distant hills. She sat gratefully in the middle of the bench set a little back from the edge.

Logan, broad-shouldered and lean-hipped, stood at the railing, every bit as captivating as the official view. He looked as cool as though he'd been for a five-minute stroll, not slogged up the same hill she had. He stepped away from the railing then sat beside her, his long legs stretched out. Too close. She moved to the edge of the bench, sat straight, her legs tucked beneath her. "Nice view," he remarked.

"You didn't come for the scenery."

"No, but I can appreciate it while I'm here." At that he lifted his sunglasses and turned and looked at her. She knew he found her physically attractive, he'd told her as much almost the first time he met her, in the same breath that he'd told her he thought her role in her country was perfectly useless. That *she* was perfectly useless but that he supposed the perfection went some way to making up for the uselessness.

Until that moment she hadn't thought him unattractive, either. He was tall with a lean strength and a ready smile and eyes that saw everything. It was that all-seeing gaze with its hidden depths that had first intrigued her. But her opinion had changed in that instant and nothing he'd done or said at their subsequent, unavoidable but blessedly brief, meetings—at the consulate or through her brother—had done anything to make her revise it.

He knew what she thought of him.

But now he, and the mocking amusement in his eyes, and his blunt way with words, and his disapproval of everything that she was, was here. Teasing her senses. Teasing *her*.

Rebecca knew enough of him, and men of his ilk, to realize that her best, almost her only, course of action was to hear him out, to at least pretend to consider what he wanted to say. "All right. I give in. You have something to say, so say it. Clearly it's the only way I'm going to get rid of you."

"I'm almost disappointed. I expected more resistance, Princess."

"I'm not going to give you a fight, Logan, but I didn't say I had any intention of taking your advice."

"Of course not."

"So?"

"Dinner?"

She stared at him.

"I'll explain my strategy to you over dinner. I know a charming restaurant not far from here."

"Why not just tell me now?"

"Because it's an...unusual strategy, and if I tell you now you're going to try to walk away without properly thinking it through. And if we've only just started eating our mains, I have a better chance of you staying to hear me out."

There was the honesty she'd come to expect from him in their few brief encounters. She could almost appreciate it. "The stomach is the way to a man's heart, not a woman's."

"I don't want your heart...only your ears. And your time."

Of course. "And once you've told me your *strategy* you'll leave me be."

"If that's still what you want."

"You have a lot of faith in your persuasiveness."

"Yes."

"But you don't know me." And nothing he could say would sway her.

"I know you well enough." He stood. "I'll pick you up at seven."

"Name the restaurant, I'll meet you there." Not only did she not want him to know where she was staying, but she also didn't want to be dependent on him for transport. Once she'd heard his so-called strategy she'd leave. On her own.

Logan smiled that too-knowing smile of his. "As you

wish, Princess," he said with mock civility. He held out his hand and without thinking she put hers in his and let him help her to standing. The touch of his palm, calloused and strong, sent an alien thrill through her that warned her that this man was like no other.

Logan looked at the woman seated across the table from him. When he'd first seen her this afternoon he almost hadn't recognized her. Dressed for the beach in a slim-fitting yellow dress with a light cardigan, her blond hair loose about her shoulders, she'd looked younger and more relaxed than he'd seen her before. He'd known a moment's regret at being the one to bring wariness and suspicion to her gaze. Now her lush hair was tied back, and she wore a fiercely elegant black, long-sleeve dress. The only thing it had going for it was that it molded nicely to her curves. But her arms were currently folded across her chest. Even without the schoolmarm dress, it didn't take an expert to read her body language.

He needed her to relax, he needed her on his side. That challenge looked even more Herculean than gaining the foothold in Europe he currently sought for his company. It had been a long while since Logan had anticipated a challenge so keenly. "Another glass of sauvignon blanc, *ma chérie?*"

"I'm not anyone's *chérie,* Logan, least of all yours."

She was her prickly, defensive best. Which might go some way to explaining why she wasn't anyone's darling, a fact that would otherwise amaze him. He knew she had her fair share of suitors but, despite press speculation, none of the relationships had ever come to anything. "So that's a yes to the wine?" He began pouring.

She was way too uptight and way too suspicious. He was taking a gamble here and he needed her a little more open-minded. A little relaxed. Had she ever been even the least bit tipsy? Hard to imagine the always restrained and regal Ice Princess giggling, maybe getting expansive and effusive. An image flashed into his mind of her head tipped back, her pale throat exposed to him, inviting the touch of his lips.

"So what's this strategy of yours?"

Logan blinked away the image, let the prim, almost grim, reality replace it. "Not until the mains."

"We've finished the appetizers. The appetizers that weren't necessary."

"But the mains haven't arrived and a deal's a deal. So tell me," he said, hoping to distract her, and perhaps himself, "what exactly were you expecting to achieve in running away from San Philippe?"

Her gray eyes, almost colorless in the dim lighting, darted away from his. "I wasn't running away. I was taking a break. A well-deserved break," she said with a note of challenge in her voice.

He liked unsettling the ever cool princess. "Call it what it is. You were running away."

"I don't have to explain myself to you."

"I was just curious to know whether there was any truth to the rumor I heard." Her posture was already perfect but somehow she managed to sit a little straighter. Confirming what he already knew, that his information was correct. After all, he had it from the best of sources.

"You shouldn't listen to gossip."

"Sometimes it pays to have my ear to the ground. I never know when I might be able to turn a situation to my advantage."

A waiter set two plates of crayfish, the New Zealand equivalent of lobster, in front of them as the wine waiter brought a new bottle to accompany this course. Logan took a sip of the chardonnay as the young man waited for his approval. "Excellent." Though to be honest, he'd rather be drinking a beer.

After their glasses were filled, Logan raised his in a silent salute to her. She watched him steadily, regally, but beneath her cool gaze he glimpsed her uncertainty. The uncertainty of someone who didn't quite know where to turn.

He could help her with that.

He set his glass down. "Assuming the gossip I've heard is true—" he watched her expressive eyes "—you will soon be somebody's *chérie* even though you don't want to be. So, I'm suggesting you…be mine."

Two

For a moment Rebecca's expression was comically blank and her pretty, royal mouth dropped open, her soft lips parting as she stared at him. Quickly, she closed her mouth and a frown wrinkled her brow. "Did you just say...? Did you suggest...?"

Logan nodded. "It's the perfect solution."

She pushed back her chair and stood. "I think I should go."

Surely that wasn't hurt clouding her eyes.

"Thank you for the meal."

Logan stood, too. He'd more or less expected that reaction, but she had the cool, serene act down to perfection and he'd wanted to ruffle those perfectly preened feathers of hers. So why did he now regret it? "Stay. Hear me out."

"I think I've heard enough."

She turned and he reached for her wrist, circling it

easily with his fingers, her skin cool beneath his touch. "Wait."

Maybe royalty really were different. Merely touching her sent a subtle charge through him. The same sensation he'd experienced up at the lookout point when she'd placed her hand in his.

She stilled and glanced at his hand but otherwise didn't acknowledge his touch, making no attempt to pull free. "Logan, we're both wasting our time here." She looked almost endearingly earnest as though she were trying to let him down gently. But her pulse beat surprisingly fast beneath his fingertips and a hint of color brushed her cheeks.

"Stay. What have you got to lose?"

She was silent a moment and he watched her searching for an answer. "An otherwise perfectly lovely evening?" she said tentatively.

He laughed lightly and held her gaze until finally her lips twitched and her gaze softened. "Stay." He released her wrist and tried not to think about wanting to coax a full smile from her. "The food's good, the setting beautiful." He gestured to the nearby ocean and she, too, looked out at the white, cresting waves, something wistful in her expression. "And otherwise I'll have to follow you. Because I only said I'd leave you be once you'd listened."

"I just don't think anything you're going to say is going to make sense."

"It'll make perfect sense once you hear it all. Just let me explain properly."

"You're not just making fun of me?"

"No." His denial was emphatic. And surprised. Her question revealed an insecurity he would never have guessed she had.

They faced off for long seconds and he could see her

hesitation, her desire to be away from him. But that desire was for more than a temporary reprieve. She wanted his absence to be permanent. Almost as much as she needed a solution to her current problem. If she wanted either of those things she needed to hear him out. And if he was to seal the deal that would secure his company's future in San Philippe he needed her to listen.

And to agree.

"I know you're used to getting your own way. But so am I. And I've had to fight far harder for it than you. I never give up." It was how he'd gotten, against everything thrown at him, to where he was now. "My way will be quicker."

Slowly, she sat. "Tell me," she said on a sigh. He could see her shutting herself off from him. Maybe that subtle withdrawal was how she got through the tedium of so many of her royal engagements.

She folded her arms across her chest. He was guessing she didn't realize how that movement subtly lifted her breasts, increasing the creamy swell at the otherwise demure neckline.

Logan brought his focus back to what he had to say. He didn't want to be noticing her breasts. He raised a forkful of crayfish to his lips, all the while keeping his gaze fixed on hers.

A flush stole up her cheeks and she looked down and picked up her fork. She was easier to disconcert than he'd expected. "Your father expects you to…wed, yes?"

She didn't say anything but she dipped her head once. Her younger brother had recently married—although he'd married the woman her father had intended for Rebecca's older brother. But her father had eventually been satisfied with the outcome. There had even been speculation that that was the match the reigning prince had intended all along. The only thing beyond speculation was the fact that he was unambiguously on record as stating he expected that soon all his children would be married.

And when Prince Henri expected something of his family, it happened.

Which meant that Rebecca and her oldest brother, Adam, were both to get married, and sooner rather than later. Off the record, her father had been even less subtle. He'd told friends that he wanted royal weddings for the morale and the economy of the country and the reputation of the royal family. And he was going to do what he needed to see that it happened.

Rebecca lifted a morsel of crayfish to her mouth. As she chewed she glanced at him in surprise. It really did taste sublime. She hadn't expected that. She took another bite and he realized that he'd stopped eating just to watch her savoring the flavors. "Admit it," he said, "I was right about the crayfish."

She sighed. "Yes."

And he knew that getting her agreement on even that small detail was important. It was a tried-and-true sales technique. Get the prospect to agree on something small—anything—and then build on that. For a time they both ate, but Logan could keep only part of his attention on his meal. The rest was on her.

She looked up, caught him watching her and set her fork down. "You were talking about my father?"

He almost regretted the switch in focus. "I believe he's even drawn up an unofficial list of suitable candidates." Rafe, Rebecca's brother, had shared that information with him one evening after a particularly close fought polo match. "And I'm on it."

"In last place," she pointed out.

"Hard to believe, I know. A few European aristocrats and assorted eager young politicians are ahead of me."

"The only difficult thing to believe is that you're on it at all. Although…I guess you could be there to make the others look good." Mischief glinted in her eyes.

Logan laughed. She sounded so sweet even as she tried to shoot him down in flames. Before tonight she'd been nothing but coolly reserved; he hadn't been on the receiving end of what was a surprisingly sharp wit. He could only assume she was unsettled by both him and her situation.

The entire thing with her father had come as a shock to him, but apparently they did things differently in San Philippe. Who was he to criticize? It was a country that would soon prove lucrative to his business interests and, more importantly, was pivotal to his plans for expanding into Europe, so hey, whatever worked for them.

"You don't want to get married?"

The glint vanished from her eyes. "Not at this point in time."

"But your father wants you to."

She inclined her head. He noted the deep plum color of her lipstick as her mouth tightened. And now, along with the image of her pale throat, another surfaced of her lips parting for him. It was only the challenge of the forbidden. All his life he'd been a rule-breaker. Living a life like hers—following *all* the rules—would destroy a part of him. He didn't know how she did it. And it wasn't his problem, either.

"You know, I think I can hear your teeth grinding."

Surprise flickered in her eyes and a reluctant smile tugged at her lips. The other thing he'd never be able to stand about the way she lived was the fact that clearly, so few people ever said what they genuinely thought to her. "Between my father and you I'm surprised I have any molars left."

She fought that hint of a smile away and looked at the slim gold watch encircling her wrist. "One more minute, Logan. That's all I'm giving you."

The thing they apparently had in common was that they both liked control. And she was fighting for it now.

It was time to stop playing games. Logan leaned forward. "You love your father, and you want to please him. You are, both literally and figuratively, his princess. Furthermore, he's not well." His failing health was another of the rumors Logan had heard. "He wants you to get married. But of all the things you *would* do for him, that's a little extreme. But the people of San Philippe want it, too, and they know he expects it. So, in short you have the pressure not only of your father's wishes, but of an entire nation watching you. You have to at least try to please him. Or be seen trying to please him."

Her gaze dipped to her watch.

"Apparently most of the candidates on your father's list, for reasons I can't begin to fathom, are practically salivating at the prospect of dating and then marrying you. I, on the other hand, don't want to get married. Least of all to someone like you."

"Flatterer." She lifted her wineglass so that it was a subtle barrier between them.

Had that been another flash of hurt? Surely not? She was the last person to care what someone like him thought. He paused. Maybe he wasn't going about this the best way. But usually being straight up worked for him, so he pressed on, watching her closely. "What I'm suggesting is that we be seen to have a relationship. We date for a time. I was thinking four intense weeks. One here, three back in San Philippe. I can fit that in before I have to be back in the States."

She took a sip of the wine.

"We'll be seen publicly together, with a few more private photos also making it into the media. It'll be clear to everyone that we're blissfully happy. In private, between our dates, we don't have to have anything to do with each other. At the end of the four weeks you'll be spotted with a diamond on the ring finger of your left hand."

"I'm supposed to fall in love with you in a matter of weeks?" Her frown deepened.

"Stranger things have happened. People see what they want to see. And if they want to see you in love, it won't be hard to imagine. Especially if you smile a little more. Don't forget nobody will know precisely when we began seeing one another. It could have been going on for some time already. Perhaps since I first saw you at the ambassador's gathering, surrounded by people but looking so remote and so alone. The night I asked for an introduction."

Her eyes widened in surprise. "You asked for that introduction?"

He nodded. He'd seen her and wanted to meet her. It had been that simple.

"And then two weeks after we get engaged," he continued, "the ring will suddenly no longer be on your finger. Our breakup will be amicable, but you'll be heartbroken." She lifted a hand to her mouth to stifle her sudden amusement. That was precisely the kind of smile he'd been thinking of for the media shots. He'd never seen her eyes dance with merriment the way they were now. It transformed her face, lifting the seriousness to reveal someone else entirely. Unfortunately, now was not when he wanted to see that reaction. "All of a sudden," he continued, "public sympathy will be back on your side and your father will see that pushing you into a relationship when you weren't ready was a mistake and that you'll need time to recover. It's got to buy you at least a year." And all of a sudden there was a glimmer of interest in those pretty gray eyes.

The interest turned just as quickly to cynicism. "What's in it for you?"

He met the suspicion in her gaze. "It'll be good for business. I'm in the process of buying out a subsidiary of leBlanc Industries. If I get it, it'll be the one that cracks Europe open for me. One of the unstated factors holding things up is that several members of the board of directors are deeply traditional and I'm seen as a newcomer with no history and not necessarily any future in the country. Dating the princess will be just what's needed to tip the scales in my favor."

"What happens when we break up?"

"We won't break up until after I have board approval and the necessary contracts are signed. All I need now is a nudge in the right direction at the right time, something to tip the scales. And if we're seen to still be friends afterward, I can manage the PR. Besides, people will take their lead from you. If you're not mad at me, no one else will have the right to be."

"So the charade would have to go on?"

"Periodically. Nothing taxing. I'll be over for business and polo anyway. All you'll have to do is smile and wave if we happen to be at the same event."

"And that's everything? That's your strategy?" She sounded far from convinced.

But that was okay because he was far from finished. "Simple but effective." People too often failed to see the strength in simplicity.

She glanced at her watch and stood. He stood, too, and

calmly endured her silent, perplexed scrutiny. Finally, she spoke. "Thank you for the meal and your honesty. It's been a truly…enlightening evening."

He sat back down and watched as she glided from the restaurant. The stillness of her head and the regal line of her back couldn't quite negate the feminine sway of her hips.

The sun peered over the horizon, spilling bright golden light onto the sea as Rebecca sat at the little linen-covered table on the balcony of the B & B. Yesterday, the chorus of birdsong and the view over the treetops and out to the ocean had captivated her. Today she was too distracted and too tired to properly appreciate the beauty. She'd had a dreadful night's sleep. For which she held Logan Buchanan and his outrageous suggestion totally responsible.

Until Logan's proposition, she'd thought—thanks to her father—that her mortification was complete.

Now Logan wanted to pretend to date her for no more reason than financial gain, expanding his systems design company into Europe. She'd have to be far more desperate than she was to consider a proposition like that.

As if she would try to deceive her father. As if anyone would believe she'd fall in love with someone like Logan, her opposite in so many ways, and in such a short space of time. Her cousin had dated his current wife for five years before getting engaged.

She wouldn't think about her brother Rafe's whirlwind romance with Lexie, his wife. The woman he'd fallen head over heels in love with. Nothing Rafe did was ever ordinary.

She knew better than to let Logan get under her skin, and yet he had. She gently slapped her hand on the table. Time to forget about him. It was over. He was gone.

Voices drifted from the room behind her. The lilting accent of Colleen, the proprietor, and someone quieter, a man whose deeper voice didn't carry so well.

Sensation tingled from her scalp and down her spine. Slowly, Rebecca turned her head. Logan lounged against the side of the open ranch slider. He wore jeans and a navy blue T-shirt and had yet to shave. He held two steaming mugs in his large hands. Dark glasses hid his eyes but a grin tugged at one side of his mouth. So male, so appealing, so…antagonizing. If only he wasn't Logan. Much as she wanted to, she didn't leap from her chair. Instead she turned back to the view. "What are you doing here?"

He strolled into her line of sight, placed a mug in front of her then hitched a hip onto the railing. "I'm staying here. It's so restful, don't you think?"

She frowned. "You followed me here last night."

"I think you'll find, Princess, that I booked in yesterday an hour or two before you."

"How did you know I was coming here?"

"This is you being stealthy?" He looked about them, shaking his head. "Put it this way, if you ever decide to take up a false identity or go on the run, get someone else to advise you."

Rebecca closed her eyes and counted silently. When she reached ten she opened them again. "Nobody, except palace security and possibly my father, if he's asked to stay briefed, knows I'm here. And I can't believe that either of them told you where I am."

"Rafe knows, too. He stayed here a year or so ago." Rafe, for reasons she couldn't fathom, was good friends with Logan. "I visited him while he was here and decided if I was ever back in the country…" He sipped his drink. "Colleen makes the best coffee. I remember that, too."

"What are you doing here—" she tapped the table "—now, annoying me?"

"I thought I'd see if you'd had time to consider my suggestion."

"It's like talking to a brick wall." Except brick walls didn't watch her with such casual nonchalance. A nonchalance that nevertheless concealed an unnerving intensity, and an implacable force of will. "I gave you my answer last night."

"You thanked me for your meal and left."

"I walked out on you." She spoke calmly, fighting a most unroyal urge to shout. Five minutes with this man and a lifetime of training went out the window.

"You needed time to think about it."

"I knew my answer by the time you'd finished your explanation."

"You can't possibly have thought it through properly. It's the perfect solution. I was sure you were smart enough to figure that out, even if it took you a few hours."

"Truly, you're astounding."

He grinned. "Why, thank you."

"It wasn't a compliment."

"Insults, compliments, it's all in the interpretation. Now, back to my suggestion."

"You can't for one minute think I'd choose to endure your company just—"

"*Endure* seems a harsh word. I thought we might even manage to have fun, particularly if we mainly do things that don't require us to talk to each other. We can attend things like the rowing regatta, where we'll sit side by side. You can occasionally lean over to whisper in my ear."

She tried to figure him out but had no idea whether he might actually be serious or was just trying to get a reaction from her. She'd seen him do that before, say deliberately provoking things guaranteed to garner a response.

She wasn't playing that game with him.

"You go right on deceiving yourself, Logan, but trust me when I say I choose my words carefully to express precisely what I mean. And spending any amount of time in your company, particularly if I was supposed to look like I was enjoying it, would be a supreme test."

"My apologies." He pulled out the chair beside her and sat down. "Go on."

He watched her closely, his dark eyes intent and looking anything but apologetic. She doubted he knew how. "I wouldn't choose to *endure* your company for any length of time in order to try to deceive my father that way." Rebecca wrapped her hands around her mug of—she glanced down at it—hot chocolate. Oh. "Thank you."

He ignored her thanks. "Your father has no qualms about trying to force you into marrying someone of his choosing."

"He'd never actually force me."

"No?"

"He might try to urge or maneuver me in certain directions."

"Sounds mighty similar to forcing."

In truth, the subtle pressures her father brought to bear did at times feel that way. But it wasn't a truth she'd admit to Logan. "No," she said lightly, "I'm used to him. I know how to deal with him. And with any other man who tries to force me, subtly or unsubtly—" she looked pointedly at Logan "—into doing things his way."

"By running away?"

She paused. "In this case, some time away from San Philippe seemed the best option. It gives us both time to think." Enough time, she was hoping, that her father would forget his schemes altogether.

"Curious."

"What's so curious about it?"

"It just doesn't seem to tally with that snippet on the internet this morning."

She shouldn't let him play her like this but she asked anyway. "What snippet?"

"He's holding an impromptu ball in your honor."

He was? There had been no talk of one before she'd left. Her father was fond of making unilateral decisions but when they concerned Rebecca he always consulted her. Almost always. Doubt gnawed at her. He just might feel strongly enough about this and would have been able to persuade himself that it was for her own good, that she'd enjoy it, just as she had the surprise parties he'd thrown for her as she was growing up. "That's no big deal," she said with a blitheness she didn't feel. "He held one for me when I turned eighteen." Eight years ago.

"Yes, but he wasn't specifically inviting San Philippe's and Europe's most eligible bachelors to that one. Was he? Marcia What's-her-name, the gossip columnist at the *San Philippe Times* is comparing it to the Cinderella story. Perhaps there's some poor bachelor out there as we speak, sitting in front of the fire amongst the cinders, polishing his half-brother's shoes and just waiting for a chance to go to the ball and win the heart of the fair princess. If only he had something to wear."

She almost smiled at the image he conjured. "Don't be ridiculous. I'm sure you're wrong. My father has said nothing about a ball to me. And inviting eligible bachelors would be far too crass." But still the doubt niggled at her. She *had* told her father she'd start at least considering potential suitors when she got back from this trip. She'd meant it to buy herself time, not for her father to go ahead and start organizing balls on her behalf.

"I suppose you're right." He pulled his phone from his pocket, scanned the screen for a few seconds and shook his head. "Marcia What's-her-name must have it all wrong. But it's right here in black and white. Actually, in color. Isn't technology marvelous."

"Show me."

"Surely you know better than to believe half of what you read in the press."

"Show me." She held out her hand.

He slid the device back into his pocket. "You'll only get upset. No doubt she'll print a retraction tomorrow."

But Rebecca knew that Marcia Roundel not only had excellent sources, but was also careful not to raise the ire of the royal family.

Colleen came out carrying two plates of breakfast and set them down on the small table.

"Thank you."

Rebecca hadn't ordered breakfast and certainly wouldn't have ordered the great stack of pancakes that had just been set before her. She opened her mouth to speak.

"This looks fabulous." Logan spoke before she could. And Colleen smiled so broadly at him and then Rebecca that she didn't have the heart to tell her she didn't want the breakfast. Usually she ate little more than a croissant or fruit and yogurt. But she could try a few mouthfuls.

"This is your doing, I take it?"

"She makes the best pancakes."

"Why is everything superlative with you? Last night's crayfish and wine were the best, her coffee's the best and now her pancakes are the best."

For a second his face clouded, the expression quickly

replaced by his usual self-assurance. "Try them and then disagree with me. I dare you."

"You have brothers, don't you? It's such a male thing, thinking if you dare someone to do something they couldn't possibly not accept the challenge. Rafe and Adam used to do it all the time."

"Three. I have three brothers. All younger than me. And daring them still works almost every time."

It was easy to imagine him in a houseful of competitive males. Rebecca looked at the stack of blueberry pancakes in front of her. "It won't be hard for you to be right this time—I've never eaten pancakes."

Logan gasped. "I knew you'd try to make me feel sorry for you. Poor little rich girl. Poor spoiled princess. But truly? No pancakes?"

"Crepes, yes. Pancakes, no."

"Crepes." He made a dismissive grunt as he pulled his chair around the table so that they sat practically shoulder-to-shoulder. He smelled good. Better even than the pancakes. Something fresh and masculine. Not meaning to, she watched the play of muscle in his arms as he reached for the jug of maple syrup. Closing large deft fingers around the small handle, he passed it to her. "You have to have maple syrup. And lots of it." For the first time since she'd seen him yesterday his focus was on something other than her. Rebecca made no move for the syrup.

He turned to look at her, his expression deadly serious. And then suddenly he smiled, a flash of white teeth, and it was like the sun coming out. Once again she pictured him as a boy with his three brothers, all of them intent on their breakfasts. She imagined laughter and arguments. Without thinking she smiled back at him.

The connection lasted no more than a second. They were

so close, both smiling, gazes locked. It was a fragment of perfection. Related to nothing, just its own small thing.

Something curious flashed in Logan's eyes, but then he blinked, the expression vanished and he leaned back in his seat, moved a little away from her. And she felt the loss. "I take my pancakes seriously."

"I picked up on that."

He turned his attention to his own breakfast. "Try them or not. It makes no difference to me." Suddenly defensive, as though in smiling at her he, too, had revealed a weakness, he shifted his chair and opened the paper Colleen had brought out with their meals. "There'll be others after me, you know, if you don't take up my offer," he said as he turned the front page.

Rebecca ignored him and tried a mouthful of syrup-drenched pancakes. They were every bit as good as she'd been led to believe. But she wasn't going to tell Logan that. He was far too sure of himself as it was. She ate almost the entire plateful before she gave up, defeated.

"What do you think?"

"They were fine."

He smiled. Not his earlier, almost boyish smile. This one knowing, unsettling and far too smug. "They were better than fine, but that's not what I was asking about."

"You can't mean your...suggestion?" What did she have to do or say to get through to him?

"That's exactly what I mean."

"Nothing you've said since last night has convinced me to change my mind."

He shook his head. "You haven't thought it through."

"Logan, you don't even like me." And she didn't care for him. He was too different, too unpredictable and unsettling.

"That's why it's the perfect solution."

She hadn't expected him to disagree with her, but still it hurt—just a little.

"You don't like me, I don't like you. If you were to try my idea with one of the other candidates on your father's list they'd undoubtedly take it wrong. They'd see it as an opportunity to get closer to you. Whereas our arrangement will be strictly regulated and strictly business."

He might have a point. But it wasn't enough.

"I have motives but they're not ulterior. And I have no feelings that can be hurt. Call me—" he stood and placed a business card on the table between them "—when you change your mind."

Rebecca didn't even have time for a royal putdown before he'd gone. Leaving a strange absence. But she didn't let herself breathe a sigh of relief until five minutes later when a solitary figure walking away from the B & B came into view on the beach, the long easy stride instantly recognizable.

Then, not touching his card, she left not only the table, but also the B & B.

And on her way out ordered herself to leave all thoughts of Logan Buchanan behind.

Three

"**Y**es. I think it could be serious." Rebecca crossed the fingers of her free hand. "Dad, I'm losing the signal. I'll tell you more about it later." As the water taxi motored toward the mainland, Rebecca turned off her phone and dropped her head into her hands.

One day. For one day she'd thought she was back in control. Admittedly a day that she'd spent looking over her shoulder half expecting Logan Buchanan to stroll out from behind the nearest tree.

Because Logan had been right, and he'd known it. Her father was hosting a ball in her honor. Under various pretexts, eligible bachelors from all over Europe had been invited. He'd denied that that was what he was doing but the denial didn't hide the facts of the guest list. And every one of the men her father considered suitable husband material for her and suitable son-in-law material for himself was on that list.

She'd received mail this morning. Colleen, far too efficient, had couriered Logan's card to her with a note that she'd left it on the table. Rebecca had thrown it out then turned around and retrieved it from the trash after Eduardo had called her. The son of a prominent San Philippe senator, Eduardo wanted to escort her to the ballet when she returned home. She'd been out twice with Eduardo several years ago. It wasn't an experience she cared to repeat. She'd formulated a diplomatic, but resolute, refusal. But mere minutes after she declined Eduardo's offer her father had called with his "wonderful" news. He also told her to expect a call from Simon Delacourte, who wanted her to accompany him to the opening of his latest jewelry store in Venice. Rebecca could think of only one way out. She told her father she was seeing someone. And when he'd asked who, she'd said Logan.

So now she just had to tell Logan himself.

Slowly, she dialed the number on the card. It was a lousy choice but he was the lesser of two evils. "It's Rebecca," she said when he answered.

"Rebecca who?"

She hung up. He knew who she was. He had to. She stared at the phone. The lesser of two evils was still evil. A second, better, thought occurred to her. She could buy herself time by just pretending to her father that she was dating Logan. Her father didn't need to know that she wasn't really, and Logan didn't need to know at all.

The perfect solution.

Ten minutes later her phone rang. "Logan here."

"Logan who?"

He laughed. "Logan Buchanan, the man you're dating."

She watched the churning wake stretching behind the boat. "I'm not dating you."

"Funny, because I just had the strangest phone call from

your father. He wants to see me as soon as I'm back in San Philippe. Apparently there's a talk he likes to have with all men who want to date his daughter."

Rebecca groaned.

"The call came through just a minute or two after you hung up on me."

"Oh." She bit back the words she wanted to utter.

"Care to enlighten me, girlfriend?"

"Don't call me that."

"Sweet thing? Punkin? *Ma chérie?*"

She could always call her father back and tell him she'd broken up with Logan.

"Is that your teeth I can hear grinding?"

Rebecca unclenched her jaw. "I'm sorry, Logan. I've made a mistake."

"I knew you'd see the error of your ways."

"Not that mistake—decision," she corrected herself. "I made one this morning when I was speaking to my father. On the spur of the moment I told him that—"

"Where are you?"

"In Russell, in the Bay of Islands." Or she would be in a matter of minutes when the water taxi docked.

"Are you going to be there for the whole day?"

She hesitated. "Yes."

"Good. I'll be there in two hours. We need to have this conversation in person. Stay where you are. Read a magazine or a book or something. I'll call you when I get there."

"No. Don't—" But it was too late. He'd hung up.

She didn't have to stay. She could just phone him back. A text came through from Eduardo suggesting they get together to discuss a charity they both sat on the board of, the pretext transparent. She didn't leave and she didn't phone Logan back. Instead she wandered around Russell, trying to enjoy the anonymity as she waited.

Her broad-brimmed sun hat shaded her face as, two hours later, she stood on the main wharf watching yachts and launches and fishing boats coming and going in the harbor. A few feet away two boys dangled fishing lines into the water. Her phone rang. Already she recognized the number. "I'm on the wharf."

"I know." The voice sounded from both her phone and from behind her.

She stayed where she was, looking out over the water as Logan come to stand beside her, casting his shadow over hers. "So this relationship we're having...?" Was that smug amusement she heard in his tone?

"I told my father I was dating you in the hope he'd cancel the ball. Apparently it's too late for that. I didn't know he'd phone you."

An old-fashioned sailing ship with rigging and square sails slid through the water toward the wharf. Men scurried over the decks and up the rigging. The ship wasn't sleek and shiny like the other boats around but it had its own charm and beauty. If she focused hard enough on it she could almost forget about the man at her side.

"It doesn't work that way, Princess. Telling him that gets you what you want but there's nothing in it for me. Plus it's a stopgap measure. With no public appearances it'll only buy you a couple of weeks at best."

"You think I don't know that. I was desperate."

"Desperate times call for desperate measures."

"So it would seem." The sailing ship—*Shanghai,* according to the faded green lettering on its side—drew up to the wharf with a grace and precision she wouldn't have thought possible from such an old craft.

"It doesn't have to be a measure taken in desperation."

Logan's voice was low and thoughtful. "You know where you stand with me. After a lifetime of subtlety and under-handed political maneuvering I'll be an uncomplicated change. I also make you look good. We're an intriguing contrast. My rugged looks with your delicate—"

"I'm still going with desperation, pure and simple." She turned to face him. Rugged? Not exactly, but there was something elementally masculine about him. He was nothing like the few men she'd dated, who all had a far more polished veneer of sophistication. Logan was tanned with a lean muscular strength. He had a look about him that said he was a man who made his own way in the world.

"Suit yourself," he said easily. "Desperation works just as well for my purposes."

A man on the *Shanghai,* with arms like Popeye, threw a rope to a teenager on the wharf. The throw went wide and Logan reached for her as she stepped out of the way and came up against him. For just a second his arm tightened around her waist, his shoulder cushioned her head and her body pressed flush against his, her back to his chest. For a second, everything within her stilled. They stepped apart at the same time and turned to watch the teen secure the heavy rope around a bollard. Rebecca used the precious minute to regain her equilibrium after the unintentional intimacy. By that time more people had gathered around them. Touching a hand to her back, Logan guided her out of the small crowd.

Farther along they stopped and watched as out in the harbor a speedboat towed a parasailor. How would it feel soaring high and fast? Too perilous for her tastes and yet here she was contemplating doing something that in its own way was just as daunting.

"I have a list of occasions I need to be seen with you

at," he said, all business. "You're welcome to add more of your own. Within limits."

"Within limits?" Oh, how the balance of power had changed.

"Yes. I don't want you getting all demanding and expecting too much. I won't do the opera and I won't go shopping with you or make nice to your sycophantic friends."

Could she push him in the water? She might lack his strength but she'd have the element of surprise on her side. He could insult her all he liked but she wasn't having him insult her friends. "My friends aren't sycophantic."

"I'm pleased to hear it, for your sake. But I still don't want to have to make nice to them. One spoiled woman is enough."

"Spoiled?"

"Admit that much at least. You're a princess, how could it be otherwise?"

Who knew? Maybe he was right. But it didn't win him any points. "Do you even think this can work?"

"Of course it can," he said with the assurance that seemed inherent in him. Did he ever doubt himself?

"But we're so different."

"That's the beauty of it. Won't it be refreshing to be with someone different? There needn't be any pretense, except in public. And who you can be honest with in return. You can say what you actually think. Nothing will offend me. Nothing will go further than me. It won't damage political relations or cause a diplomatic uproar. Try it."

It was almost tempting. But she'd had a lifetime of keeping her thoughts hidden. And much as she might get some kind of pleasure from pointing out to Logan just how overbearing he was being, not to mention insulting, she wasn't going to do it. She couldn't.

He nudged her with his elbow. "Go on. You can do it. I'll bet you've got a long list of fancy words you'd like to call me. Tell me I'm insufferable and deplorable. You know you want to. I've never been called names by a princess."

"That's the difference between you and me. Good manners. Breeding, some might say."

He looked sharply at her, then guided her out of the way of a kid on bicycle heading straight for them. "What do you know about me?"

They strolled to the other side of the wharf. "I know you're a successful entrepreneur, your primary business is systems design but you have diversified business interests in many countries. But not, I think, New Zealand. And I know you're a friend of Rafe's—which, trust me, is not in itself a recommendation. I also know you think monarchy is an outdated and elitist concept. And that's everything. Apart from the fact that you think extremely highly of yourself. So all in all I know very little. Which is all the more reason to make what you're proposing and I seem to be considering ridiculous."

"You've gone past the stage of considering if you've told your father you're seeing me."

"But only just past it. I'm definitely still in the 'perhaps I've made a mistake and should back out' stage. Is there more I should know before I get any further into this?"

"You mean am I going to give you the reason or excuse you need not to do this? No. I'm certainly not the type of man you've dated before. My background's not great, very common, very poor, in fact, but there's nothing seriously unsavory in it. Nothing that will reflect badly on you."

"I'm pleased to hear it."

"So, let's get this show on the road. We need somewhere private where we can discuss the terms of our arrangement."

"Terms? There are going to be terms?"

"Of course. Think of it as setting out our mutual agreement."

"That's insane. We're only going to be pretend dating."

"But we both need to be clear on what we expect. Because it's not dating. I want all the parameters in place. It's for your own protection as well as mine."

A middle-aged woman on the wharf ahead of them nudged her partner and pointed at Rebecca. As her partner lifted a camera, Logan deftly turned Rebecca around.

He took her hand and walked her toward the land end of the wharf. "I thought you'd want people getting shots of us." She'd half expected to be ambushed by photographers the instant Logan had appeared at her side.

"I do. But not until you've said yes unequivocally. Not until you've admitted to yourself that this is what you need and want to do. After that there will undoubtedly be photos. Lots of them."

"So you're not going to just bully me into this by making it seem the only option?" Did he know he still held her hand? His larger, calloused fingers engulfed hers, his self-assurance evident in even his grip. He was clearly too used to taking control, and she would have to be vigilant about protecting her own interests. No one else was going to do it for her.

"It's not your only option but it is your best option. I've thought it through from both of our points of view. It has to be a win-win situation or it'll never work. But the sooner it starts the sooner it's over. Where are you staying?"

Rebecca sighed. He was right. Delaying beginning only delayed the end. Once they broke up she would be given space and privacy and most importantly time. "Friends have a place on one of the islands."

"George and Therese? I thought they were in South America."

Of course he knew them. Though Therese was one of Rebecca's best friends, George was one of Rafe's. And if Rafe knew them, then odds were that Logan did, too. "They are."

"I'll come out there with you now. A little privacy while we get this hammered out will be a good thing. I want our public appearances carefully planned."

"And no more than necessary."

"My thoughts exactly. See, we're on the same page already. We'll be able to make this work."

For the first time a flicker of hope replaced the desperation. Maybe they really could make it work.

One hour later, shaded by an enormous market umbrella, they sat on sun loungers by the pool. Though summer was officially over, it lingered on in the balmy temperatures. Rebecca, wearing shorts and a loose blouse, sat more upright than Logan with a notepad on her lap and a pen in her hand. Logan had a notepad, too—she'd given it to him. The difference being that his was lying on his face to block the light.

For a man who was reported to work intensely seven days a week, he was currently a picture of relaxation.

"I'll want you with me at my father's ball," she said, doing her best to ignore the expanse of muscled torso hinted at beneath the T-shirt that stretched across his shoulders and chest. *Unfair,* she'd wanted to protest. That, too, was a difference between him and the men she'd dated, this lean purposeful strength that looked to have been honed over a lifetime of activity. He even had a couple of small, intriguing scars, one on a bicep, another across a knuckle. She clenched her hands. She did *not* wonder how her fingertips would feel on those scars or the contours of his chest…

He lifted the notepad from his face and looked at her as he shook his head. "That's too far away. I'll be back in the States by then. I'm speaking at a charity fund-raiser the day before."

"I want you with me at my father's ball. Can you come back for it?" He watched her closely, frowning slightly as he appeared to consider her request. "That's my deal breaker. Remember, Logan—" she smiled as she quoted his own words "—it has to be a win-win for both of us."

"Okay," he said slowly then lowered the papers back to his face, "I'll come back for it."

"These things you want to be seen with me at." She scanned the list, which, as well as dinners at elite restaurants and high-profile gatherings, included black water rafting—she didn't even know what that was—and a polo match.

"Mmm-hmm."

"They're not my usual type of thing. I generally live as quiet a life as I can outside of royal commitments."

"If we did your usual thing no one would seriously believe I was dating you. But you can add your *things* to the list, bearing in mind there's only so much of the orchestra and inane cocktail parties that I can stand." He sat up, placing his feet on either side of the sun lounger, and suddenly he was intense. "Are we doing this or not? Because if it's not, pleasant as this is, I have other places to be. And you, doubtless, will be wanting to come up with another plan to put your father off. Unless of course you want to start working your way through his list?"

He held her gaze. The lesser of two evils? Suddenly she wasn't so sure.

"It's a good plan," he said.

Rebecca swallowed. "I'm in." And with those two tiny words she committed herself to the unknown.

Four

Logan had had some bad ideas in his time. He hadn't thought this was one of them.

Until now.

He dragged his gaze from Rebecca's curves as she wriggled into the full-length, skintight wet suit and reached behind her back for the zipper. He'd known that beneath the sleek lines of her tailored outfits she had a good body. But the wet suit wasn't tailored.

It clung. Like a second skin.

And it left nothing to the imagination. He was, he admitted, floored. *Good* was a completely inadequate word.

Suddenly he wanted her back in something—anything—that disguised the curve of breast and waist, and flare of hip, the length of her slender legs. Failing that, he wished their guides, standing close in the sparsely furnished briefing room, were a mile away because he'd seen the appreciative glances the young men had directed at her, even as they were explaining the seriousness of their safety procedures.

And that was before the wet suit.

It wasn't that he was being either possessive or protective, it was just that...she seemed to have no idea. Not of how she looked or of how others looked at her. She thought they saw only the princess—not a woman.

The black water rafting—floating on inner tubes through an underground cave system—had been his idea, in part because he'd figured that it would be something completely different for her, something a little out of her comfort zone. And he didn't want her thinking she was the one in control.

Now she was the one making *him* uncomfortable.

She turned her back to him and stepped in front of him. "Can you finish pulling my zip up, please." She sounded exasperated. The zipper rested in that hard-to-reach spot between her shoulder blades, revealing a deep vee of pale skin.

Logan closed his eyes and swallowed. Opening his eyes, he rested one hand on the curve of her waist as he slid the zipper up, closing the vee, sealing away the skin with a mixture of relief and regret.

"Thank you." She stepped away and he let go of the breath that had stayed trapped in his lungs.

He forced his attention back to the guides as they explained what to expect during their trip.

Ten minutes later the four of them stood at the top of a short drop into a dark, watery cavern. The first guide jumped in, landing with a splash. Rebecca, who was supposed to jump in next, took off her headlamp hard hat and fiddled with the adjustment for the chin straps before placing it back on her head.

Was it his imagination or was she looking paler than she had earlier? Logan moved to stand in front of her. He shifted her cold, fumbling fingers out of the way and fastened the strap for her, his fingers brushing her throat and beneath her chin. "Are you okay?" he asked quietly. "We don't have to do this if you don't feel good about it." He'd wanted her out of her comfort zone, but he hadn't meant to frighten her. And fear was what he thought he read in her wide gray eyes. He had to remember that she was sheltered and probably pampered—she was nothing like his brothers, relishing challenges, relishing the chance to vie for superiority. Never backing down.

Not meeting his gaze, she stepped away from him and smiled. But it was a royal smile. Brittle and practiced. "I'm fine." Before he could say anything more she took hold of her inner tube, took a deep breath and stepped off the ledge.

Maybe not so dissimilar to his brothers.

Only much better looking.

She bobbed, seated on her inner tube and floating out of the way as Logan jumped into the frigid water after her, followed by their second guide.

In the quiet, watery darkness, they drifted together through the caves, holding on to one another's inner tubes as their headlamps played over the vaulted caverns adorned with ancient stalactites and stalagmites. The only sound was the occasional drip of water falling from the ceiling above.

They passed through a narrow opening and into a much larger cavern. And on the lead guide's instruction turned off their headlamps. Beside him, Rebecca gasped.

He shared her wonder. The darkness would have been complete but for the tiny lights of thousands of glowworms dotting the unseen limestone surfaces and reflecting in the ink-black water. As it was, he could see nothing of the hand he held up inches from his face.

It was like floating in the night sky.

Rebecca shifted her grip on his inner tube and her hand bumped into his. When she would have shifted her hand away again he took hold of it. He couldn't make out so much as her outline. But the joining of their hands, palm to palm, was a warm point of human contact amid the silent wonder. They maintained that wordless contact for the next twenty minutes of their trip.

It wasn't until they floated out of the darkness and into the light and warmth of day that Rebecca eased free of his grip.

They reached the point where they got out of the water. Logan went first and again held out his hand. "Did you enjoy it?" he asked.

She let him help her from the water. "It was certainly the most unusual first date I've ever been on."

"But did you enjoy it?" he persisted, not accepting her evasion. "It's not a contest, Princess, you don't lose anything by telling me you enjoyed it."

She sighed. "It was amazing. Thank you. I never would have done it otherwise." Gratitude, and traces of their shared wonderment, shined in her eyes.

"You were frightened? At the start?"

"I was...uncomfortable."

Was that princess-speak for terrified? "I'm sorry. I didn't know."

She smiled at him, her regal best. "You weren't supposed to."

Admiration wasn't something he'd expected, or wanted, to feel for her. Nor, he admitted, was the attraction that had him thinking extremely improper thoughts about the very proper princess. The admiration couldn't hurt. The attraction, on the other hand, could well lead him into trouble.

Three days later Rebecca sat with Logan in the plush cabin of his private jet as they flew to San Philippe. News had filtered through to the media that she had been spotted with a mystery man, so they were expecting something of a photographers' welcoming party. She'd even been reported on one site as "cavorting with her new beau at an island retreat." Rebecca, who knew better than to get upset by anything in the media, had taken exception to the use of the word *cavorting*. She never cavorted, and walking along the surf's edge with someone, as she'd done with Logan twice at George and Therese's place, hardly counted as such. Next thing they'd say was that she'd been canoodling.

She finished reading through her notes on her next week's schedule and looked at the man reclining in the armchair across from her as he worked at his laptop, large fingers moving surprisingly deftly over the keyboard, a frown of concentration etching two vertical lines above his nose.

There was no cavorting or canoodling when they were in private. Their relationship was, as agreed, strictly business. In fact, he barely spoke to her. Occasionally she caught him looking at her but his expression revealed nothing of what he thought. And occasionally she caught herself looking at him. Sometimes in an effort to try and figure him out. Sometimes in reluctant fascination.

Upon landing they would part ways and she'd see him

tomorrow for the ballet. Something he'd made clear he wasn't looking forward to. The jet taxied to a halt and Logan shut down his laptop and looked at her. "Are you ready for this?"

"Not really." It didn't feel right. On so many levels. "I've never tried to trick people before."

He stowed the laptop in its case and stood. "What, you've never pretended you were happy when you were actually seething mad, or pretended to look interested when you were bored out of your skull? Never pretended you were fine when you were frightened?"

"Well, yes, but this is different." She made no move to unfasten her seat belt.

Logan nodded at the novel open in her lap. "How long do you think you can hide out in the jet for?"

Reluctantly, she closed the book and slipped it into her tote. "I'm not usually the center of media speculation. That's traditionally been Rafe's role because he was the one getting into scrapes, or Adam's because he's heir to the throne."

He held a hand toward her. "Come on, Princess. I've seen you work vast cheering crowds."

She looked at his hand.

He followed her gaze. "You may as well get used to it." The fact that she *was* getting used to it was part of her problem. He offered his hand with such unthinking ease, as though it were a perfectly normal thing to do. Just another sign of the differences between them. In her world nothing could be done, or said, without thought for the consequences, for the appearances, for the interpretations and implications.

She took the offered hand—still there was that little frisson of sensation that ought to have gone by now—and let him help her to standing, and they walked toward the door. "This'll be a cinch," he said. "We get off the jet, we smile, we wave. A quick kiss. We get in the waiting car together but it drops you off at the palace and takes me to my hotel. We don't see each other again until I pick you up for the ballet."

Rebecca had been analyzing—again—how it felt to rest her hand in his. It was different, but not unpleasant. His firm, dry grip was certainly more appealing than Eduardo's somewhat clammy grip. "Back up a second. What did you say?"

"You go to the palace, I go to my hotel. And then I'll pick you up tomorrow night for the ballet."

They'd reached the open doorway at the top of the stairs and as predicted a crowd had gathered behind a roped-off area.

"That wasn't the bit I meant."

"You meant this, no doubt." He smiled and waved at the crowd and then he slipped an arm around her shoulders, pulled her toward him, bent his head to hers and kissed her—stealing her breath, along with rational thought and the strength in her knees.

Heat.

It scorched through her. His lips were gentle and seeking and in that first surprised instant she forgot to pull back, forgot to analyze, and instead gave herself to the kiss, let herself experience it, the touch of his lips to hers an intimate joining. His warmth surrounded her. His arm around her back shielded and supported her. And held her close. She let herself enjoy—

Enjoy? No.

She pulled back and recognized the sound of a cheer from the crowd. What on earth had she just done?

Logan's gaze sought hers. Something serious in those dark eyes quickly transformed into amusement. He winked.

"Not so icy after all, Princess. In fact, not bad for a first kiss. You tensed up a little at the end, but we can work on that."

"First and last. We won't be *working* on anything." She searched for the *ice* he accused her of. Her refuge. Her armor. She was desperate that he not know that inside she was a shaken mess and anything but icy.

He took her hand and together they descended the steps.

"Last? That'll never convince anyone. I can't let you be right about that."

"The cavorting was bad enough," she said, relieved that the words came out with just the right touch of distance. He laughed, just as he had when he'd first realized her outrage over that word. "I have a reputation and an image to maintain, both while you're here and after you've gone. And I don't think—"

He kissed her again, quick and hard, and came up smiling broadly. "Good. Don't think. Some things are better that way." Dimly, she heard another cheer from the crowd. "That's tomorrow's papers taken care of," he said easily. "I have a reputation to consider, too."

She couldn't push him away, that wouldn't look right at all, and she definitely couldn't touch her fingers to her lips. She withdrew her hand from his, lifted her chin and continued to the bottom of the stairs, Logan at her side.

And she just knew he was smirking.

The chauffeur shut the door behind him and Logan waited. The princess sat on the far side of the seat from him—as far as she could get in the confines of the luxury car. Her gaze—part irritation, part contemplation—was fixed straight ahead as she fed the strap of her handbag back and forth through her fingers. A small frown drew her finely arched eyebrows closer together.

Logan leaned back, crossed one foot over the other and laced his fingers behind his head. Doubtless she'd have something to say about the kiss.

Finally her fingers stilled. She pressed the button that raised the privacy screen and turned to him. "About that kiss."

He smiled.

"It wasn't funny."

"No. It definitely wasn't funny. Intriguing, I would have said. There was distinct potential." And though he was deliberately trying to needle her, he spoke the truth. The kiss, her flash of response, the taste of her, had hit him harder than he could have imagined, had tempted him, had him wondering. "I think with a little practice you'll—"

"We agreed we were going to be seen together. We didn't talk about kissing." Her tone was wintry and controlled, as though at any moment she was going to issue a royal edict banishing him to the Arctic or wherever people from San Philippe got banished to.

"You want people to believe we're in a relationship, don't you?"

"Yes, but…" She looked away, suddenly uncertain.

"But what?"

"Surely we can achieve that without kissing."

"No, we can't. I'll look like your bodyguard or a brother. And that's not the look I'm aiming for."

"We could hold hands and look lovingly at one another."

"We'll be doing that, too."

"Though the looking lovingly is going to be a struggle," she said with feeling as she glared at him. Nothing remotely loving there.

"We'll manage. Listen, Princess. I didn't enjoy it any more than you." At least, he knew he shouldn't have.

Her frown deepened. Clearly she thought he ought to

have enjoyed it and only she had the right to complain. "It's one of those tasks we'll have to endure."

Her jaw worked for several seconds. "Then there need to be some parameters."

"Such as?" He turned more fully toward her. "This ought to be good. Royal kissing rules."

"Only in public."

He nodded. "Fair enough."

"And there should be a time limit."

"Makes sense. Forty-five seconds? A minute?"

She turned to look at him. "Good gracious, no."

His gaze dipped to her lips—the lips in question. Today they were a soft pink that matched the silk of her blouse. Silk that had shifted beneath his hands as he'd held her shoulders to kiss her. "Too short. You'd like more? I guess I can work with that."

"This is no time for joking. I was thinking a maximum of five seconds."

"Now who's joking?"

"I'm perfectly serious."

She certainly looked it, her wide gray eyes intent. But she had to be having him on. "Who kisses for five seconds? I've seen my grandparents kiss for longer. Though," he added, "it was an image that stayed with me for a disturbingly long time."

She said nothing.

"Seriously. Who kisses for five seconds? Your first kiss behind the bike shed at school maybe." But then again she'd probably been to an all-girls school that didn't have a bike shed. Just a limo parking area.

Her gaze went to the window and her fingers again began working at the strap of her handbag.

"Who was the last man you dated, Princess?" Now he was curious. It'd be easy enough to find out. Doubtless there were entire gossip columns devoted to the subject. "Some namby-pamby royal hanger-on?"

"My dating history is nothing you need to know about. You're getting sidetracked. I'll go as high as ten seconds. No more."

"I can have you begging for more."

"You flatter yourself, Logan. Ten seconds will be all I can stomach and I'll be counting every one of those."

"Is that a dare, Princess? A challenge? I've told you how seriously the men in my family take a challenge."

"It was a statement of fact. I'm just warning you. Don't take it as anything else."

"Ten seconds is scarcely enough time to get started."

"You seem to be forgetting that we'll only be kissing to perpetuate a myth. It's not as though we'll really be kissing."

"And when we're eating together are we only going to pretend to eat the food? Pretend to enjoy the food?" he asked.

"No. Of course we'll be eating and if it tastes good…"

"My point exactly."

"But if we're not enjoying the meal we still have to look like we are," she said, desperately trying to regain ground in this conversation. "And we won't prolong meals unnecessarily."

He slid his arm along the backseat of the car, slipped his hand beneath the fall of her blond hair and ran his thumb along her jaw. She tensed beneath his touch, sat a little straighter. "I'm not sure whether you're just trying to fool me or whether you're fooling yourself, as well. I've been watching you." Again he caressed her jaw with his thumb. He waited to see whether she'd move away from his touch. She didn't, but she was doing her best to ignore it. Maybe it was only him who was struggling. Her skin was so soft it invited touch. "You're more tactile than I'd first thought. You like to touch things, textures and shapes. I saw you in that art gallery in New Zealand and in the gift shop afterward. You felt the silks, ran your fingertips over the pottery, you closed your eyes when you sniffed the soaps. And I'm guessing there's a far more sensual nature beneath the cool exterior than you let on."

"You're wrong. I'm naturally cool and reserved and I like it that way."

"I'd say you're naturally passionate and sensuous and you've trained yourself not to reveal it. You keep your thoughts and feelings hidden, but that doesn't mean you don't have them."

He had to stop. He didn't want to be thinking about her as passionate, it was easier—necessary even—to safely categorize her as the cool, reserved woman she categorized herself. Haughty even, that was how he'd thought of her since he'd first met her. Remote. Unfeeling.

But there'd been nothing haughty about the way she'd clung to his hand in the caves, and *haughty* had been the furthest word from his mind when he'd seen her in that full-length wet suit, seen the sensuous curves that were usually hidden beneath tailored skirts and blouses like the one she wore now.

And there had been nothing remote or unfeeling about their kiss.

If he wasn't careful he'd find himself orchestrating public occasions at which to kiss her. And he'd take every one of his allotted seconds. And more. Though who'd be being taught a lesson, her or him, he wasn't entirely sure.

He withdrew his hand from the vulnerable curve of her neck, and dropped it to the seat. Strictly business, he had to remember that, focus on the ultimate goal, buying the subsidiary he needed. That was what mattered here.

The car eased to a stop beneath the hotel's portico.

As the doorman opened his door Logan saw a posse of photographers standing in waiting. "See you tomorrow, *ma chérie*."

"Don't—"

He touched a finger to her lips, then replaced the finger with his mouth, felt her soft, made-for-kissing lips part with a yielding gasp of surprise. So much more mobile than when she was arguing with him.

He didn't have time to savor the taste or feel of her before he lifted his head. "Five seconds." Or thereabouts. He'd lost count after one second but had definitely kept it short. "Short enough for you? I'll work on the getting-you-to-beg-for-more kisses later."

He exited the car, waved to the photographers and strolled into the hotel.

Five

The tower clock chimed the hour as Rebecca stepped into the blue room at the palace and stopped. Logan, his back to her, stood in front of the window that overlooked the manicured gardens.

She'd had time to gather her thoughts after their... encounters on the steps of the plane and in the car. And she knew he was toying with her. Yes, he was more experienced than she was, but she was no fool.

Slowly, he turned and they surveyed each other. He wore an expertly tailored tuxedo that highlighted a physique that needed no highlighting. The change, after the jeans and T-shirts of the past week, was an intriguing, almost breath-stealing contrast. If she were the sort to have her breath stolen.

As if in defiance of the refinement of the tux, his bow tie dangled untied around his neck and a five o'clock shadow darkened his jaw. He didn't look like any man she'd ever dated.

Or any man she'd ever known.

A raw masculinity always lurked beneath the surface.

He dominated the room, seeming to dwarf the antique furnishings, making them look flimsy and overly ornate. But it was more than just his size—he had a presence, a sheer force of will that cloaked him. He would never blend in or fade into the background as some people did. She'd once walked in on Eduardo in this same room and taken far too long to realize he was even in it.

Yet she couldn't let Logan exercise that will on her or she'd find herself trampled. Most people kept their distance from her, and she relied on that fact. Logan seemed to want to push boundaries. It was in his nature. But now that he'd made her aware of that with his kisses, she was better prepared to deal with him. The kisses had caught her off guard. That was the only reason she'd found herself responding, almost…wanting. His arm, powerful yet gentle as he'd swept it around her shoulders, pulling her to him, against him, had made her feel—

"Princess." Logan nodded.

Her thoughts snapped back to the present and the decision she'd made to maintain her distance from him, to show him she was in control of herself, at least. She'd quickly realized she'd never have a hope of exercising any control over Logan. "Are you always going to call me that?" She hated the formality of that label coming from him, carrying, as she knew it did, his unflattering sentiments on royalty.

"I thought you'd ruled out Sweet Thing and Punkin?"

She met the challenge in his dark gaze. "I was thinking *Rebecca* might do."

"Or Becs or Becky?"

"Or just Rebecca," she said, patiently refusing to react.

"No."

"No?"

"It's not right. I'm not sure what is. I'll let you know when I figure it out."

"How can you tell me my name's not right and that you'll let me know when you figure out what is? It's *my* name. Who are you to say otherwise?"

"My apologies." He paused. "Princess. Forgive my presumption." One side of his mouth quirked up in a grin. He was enjoying himself immensely, getting pleasure from riling her.

"I'll *let you know* when you're forgiven." She couldn't help but respond to that grin. "In the meantime we ought to get going."

Logan crossed to her and held out his arm.

"Your bow tie." She gestured to the dark strip of fabric that dangled around his neck. "Do you want me to call someone to tie it for you?"

His eyes narrowed on her and he lifted his hands, buttoned the top button of his dress shirt and with practiced movements began tying the bow. "Is there a mirror in here?" he asked when he was all but done.

"No."

He finished the knot. "Is it even?"

"Almost. You just need to tug that side—" she pointed to left of the bow "—out a little."

He adjusted it but unbalanced it the other way. He looked at her and she shook her head.

"Could you?" he asked. "It's tricky without a mirror." She could see in his eyes that he expected her to refuse.

Rebecca hesitated then stepped closer. Apparently she was little better than his brothers at turning down an unspoken dare.

He'd helped her with her chin strap at the rafting, this was no different. Only then she hadn't been quite so aware of the breadth of his chest or his scent. He hadn't been wearing the cologne—citrusy and subtly spicy—that he wore now.

Nor, then, had he yet kissed her.

So she hadn't been thinking of his lips, the precise full shape of them. And she wouldn't now. She reached up, the back of her hands brushed the underside of his jaw and she felt the gentle abrasion of hours-old beard. She pulled her hands away and stepped back, ignoring his grin.

"Perfect," she said, focusing her gaze on the black bow tie.

"Thank you. You're not too bad yourself."

"I was referring to the bow tie."

"And I was referring to you. You look…beautiful."

Rebecca opened her mouth, suddenly lost for words at the sincerity in his voice and eyes.

She'd spent an inordinately long time deciding what to wear this evening. As a princess her dress was scrutinized at the best of times. But tonight she had to send the right message to the public and be careful not to send the wrong message to Logan. She didn't want him to think she'd dressed for him. After trying on innumerable outfits she'd gone back to her first choice—a simple ice-blue gown beaded with tiny crystals. It had a scooped neckline at the front and at the back it dipped rather more daringly. The slim-fitting skirt fell to the floor with a slit in the side— nothing too revealing—that allowed her to walk.

"Thank you," she said quietly. Please don't let that be a blush she could feel heating her face.

He held out his arm. "Shall we?"

Rebecca hesitated then looped her arm through his, felt the fabric of his suit shift over the muscles of his forearm.

"You spoke to my father this morning?" she asked, as much to distract herself from his nearness as anything else.

"Yes. And he warned me, very diplomatically, that if I hurt you in any way I'll suffer the consequences of his enduring wrath."

She nodded. "He has that talk with anyone who wants to date me."

"It's very effective."

"You're not…"

"No. It'd take more than that to scare me off."

"You wouldn't be the first one." Several relationships she'd had hopes and dreams for had faltered at that hurdle.

He glanced at her. "Then the ones who were scared off weren't worthy."

"Thank you. But you do remember that for our plan to work I need to look heartbroken. Dad could turn people against you."

"I remember. But our breakup will be mutual. You'll assure him of that. And I'll be just as heartbroken as you," he said lightly. "Though of course I'll hide it better."

She sat in the Ferrari's passenger seat. "I usually have a royal car take me to formal engagements like this one."

"And I prefer to drive. I like the control."

"Figures."

His lips twitched.

What it meant for Rebecca was that rather than being the width of a broad seat away from him she was the width of a gear stick away. And dependent on him. On the plus side it meant that, with his hands occupied with the steering wheel and gearshift, he couldn't slide his hand behind her neck as he'd done yesterday in the car. Couldn't disconcert her that way.

He pulled to a stop in front of the royal theater house.

A valet opened her door and Rebecca got out. It was also harder to exit a low-slung Ferrari with the appropriate royal dignity than it was a limousine. But she managed.

Logan tossed his keys to the valet and approached, his gaze narrowed intently on her, seeming to focus on her lips, and a smile played about his eyes.

"Don't even think about it," she whispered as he stopped in front of her.

"About what?"

"You were going to kiss me."

Dark eyebrows lifted. "Actually, no, but if it's what you want."

Had he not been intending to kiss her? Was that her imagination? "It's not what I want," she insisted. "We've already kissed enough."

"Was that in the Royal Kissing Rules, frequency as well as duration? I'm sure I don't remember."

"You remember."

He reached for her hand, and interlaced his fingers with hers. An intimate joining, his larger fingers stretching hers apart. "A curious question, Princess. So if I understand it—" they began walking the stairs to the grand, arched building "—in your world, lovers kiss for no more than five seconds and no more than once a day?"

"No, but…we're not lovers."

"It's what we want people to think, isn't it?"

"No," she said more abruptly than she'd intended, something like fear making her blurt the word out.

He stopped walking and turned to her. "No?"

"They can…wonder, they can perhaps guess or assume but…"

He leaned closer. "So they can wonder if when I get you home—" his words were low, barely more than a whisper "—I'll be peeling this beautiful dress off your exquisite body, baring your pale skin to the moonlight and touching my hands, my lips—"

"Stop it."

Behind a cordoned-off area flashes were popping wildly as they stood halfway up the stairs having a conversation in which she was completely out of her depth.

"What is it that frightens you, *ma chérie?*" As if sensing her desire to run, his hand tightened around hers. "No one is close enough to hear."

Out of her depth and getting deeper. "Nothing frightens me," she lied.

"Nothing? Oh, to be you."

"Logan." She tugged at his hand. "Now isn't the time or the place."

"Perhaps not."

Slowly he turned and Rebecca used the opportunity to disengage her hand. Which only meant that as they reached the top of the stairs and approached the door he could lift his hand to her back, rest warm, blunt fingers along her spine. The images that she'd conjured in her mind—Logan peeling off her dress, touching her skin with those large calloused hands—returned, sending a bolt of unwanted yearning through her.

The ballet was… Rebecca couldn't say what it was. She barely knew which ballet was being performed, and she couldn't say whether it was being performed well. It was the royal ballet company so one could make assumptions, but her lack of focus had been complete. Logan—his words, his actions, his proximity—prevented coherent thought. Though she'd refused to look at him through the first act of the ballet, all her thoughts were on him, the way he disconcerted her—deliberately—as he'd done tonight. The way he took what should have been ordinary conversation and twisted it. The way he made her think thoughts she didn't want to think. The way just his fingers interlaced with hers made her think of other joinings and interlacings.

He had her—usually serene and in control—tied in knots, and she didn't know how to manage it, how to untangle herself, or her thoughts.

At a small sound beside her she turned. Logan sat low in his seat, his head tipped back and his eyes…closed! The sound had been a gentle snore. It had also caught her sister-in-law's attention. Lexie, sitting on Logan's other side, looked from Logan to Rebecca and then, suppressing a grin, returned her attention to the ballet. Lexie might think it funny but Adam, here with the Swedish ambassador's daughter, would not. He took his duties seriously. Some would say too seriously, the weight of his future responsibilities already weighing heavily. It had been a long time since she'd heard her brother's laughter and the last thing she wanted to do was call down his censure on her now.

Rebecca elbowed Logan in the arm. Slowly, he opened his eyes, then narrowed them on her. "What was that for?"

"What was it for? You were sleeping," she hissed. She'd never hissed in her life.

"I wasn't sleeping. I was reliving one of those beautiful earlier moments in my head."

"You were snoring."

Even in the dim light of the theater she could see the amusement in his eyes as he feigned interest and asked, "So, this new lead dancer…what do you think of her?"

Rebecca turned back in her seat.

"Nice legs."

"You're not supposed to be looking at her legs."

"I meant yours."

She looked down to see that with her twisting in her seat the side split in her dress had ridden up and parted, revealing a glimpse of her thigh. Which was still vastly more than she wanted Logan looking at. She rearranged the dress so that it sat properly.

He leaned closer. "I'm still imagining taking it off you."

Maybe she shouldn't have woken him.

At the intermission he took her hand and walked with her to the royal lounge. When he would have approached a cluster of people that included her brothers and Eduardo she steered him instead to a quiet corner of the room.

Still holding her hand, he turned to her. "You want to make out? Here? Do you think that's really appropriate?"

He took far too much pleasure in needling her. "It'd be more appropriate than me killing you. Here." She tried to slide her hand from his but his grasp tightened.

"So you do want to make out?" His gaze dropped to her lips then flicked to the split in her dress before coming back to connect with hers. Deliberately provocative. He rubbed his thumb over the back of her hand.

"No. But I do want to kill you," she said, smiling sweetly for the benefit on any watchers.

"Because?" His thumb probed gently between her fingers.

And Rebecca had to fight to keep her focus on what she was saying and not on what he was doing. "You fell asleep. And you made me hiss."

"Bet I can make you sizzle, too."

"Be serious." She didn't want to contemplate that assertion for fear that he might be right. "We're talking about you falling asleep during the ballet."

"And that's a capital offense in San Philippe?"

"I'm a patron of the ballet," she said in a low voice.

"I'm so sorry."

For a moment she almost believed he was sincere in

his regret. He took two champagne flutes from a hovering waiter and passed one to her.

"That must be awful for you. Do you have to come very often?"

"I love the ballet."

"You do?" For the first time this evening she knew she was hearing genuine sentiment—surprise—in his question.

Eduardo appeared at Logan's side. She'd been so intent on Logan that she hadn't seen him approach. "Rebecca." He nodded and gave a small tight smile. "Logan."

She knew the two men had met previously. She just didn't think they'd got along. Even looking at them now, and even both good-looking and dressed in tuxedos, they were polar opposites. Eduardo lean and fair, Logan with his darker coloring and more powerful build.

"How are you enjoying the ballet, Logan? I wouldn't have thought it was your thing." Eduardo had been raised in the same circles she had, privileged and cultured—a world away from the blue-collar background Logan had told her a little of, and of which he was so proud. Eduardo was basically a decent man when things were going his way, but he could be cold and calculating and could, at times, be a complete and utter prat. She had the feeling now might be one of those times. She'd refused his offer to accompany her to this very ballet.

Logan darted a glance at Rebecca, amusement in those dark eyes of his, and she tried to convey with her gaze that she needed him to take this seriously. Her family and friends, many surreptitiously watching, needed to be convinced that they really were in a relationship. That they had things in common.

"I'm enjoying it almost as much as I'm enjoying Becs's company." Hopefully only she knew that meant not at all.

"Becs?" Eduardo repeated disapprovingly, echoing Rebecca's surprise. Logan moved so that he stood beside her. He lifted his hand and touched the bare skin of her back, sending a shiver coursing through her. She couldn't step away from the touch without destroying the image they wanted to create. And a part of her—a small rebellious part—didn't want to. His fingers were warm and gentle. His touch possessive. Rebecca took a sip of champagne.

Eduardo looked intently at Logan for long seconds. "I heard you two were an item," he said. "I'll admit I didn't believe it until I saw you here together."

"We ran into each other in New Zealand. Becs hasn't been able to tear herself from my side since." His fingers trailed up and down her spine. He couldn't know the strange effect that movement had on her, causing heat to coil and swirl low within her. She tried to ease just a little away from him, but he spread his fingers and pulled her in closer. She felt the imprint of his palm and of each fingertip. She couldn't be certain but she thought perhaps those fingertips had slipped beneath the edge of the back of her dress. And again, that image that he'd planted outside on the steps, of him peeling her dress off, came back to her. Those large calloused hands of his that she knew, from watching him at his laptop and tying his bow tie, could also be deft and clever.

Rebecca swallowed another sip of champagne and marshaled her errant thoughts as she tried to force the heat from her face. "He's joking, of course. Logan does so love to twist things. He's the one who can't seem to let go of me. I was scarcely aware of him until he invited me to dinner that first night."

"Ahh, but you're aware of me now, aren't you, *ma chérie?*" His thumb circled slowly.

Far too aware.

Rebecca's gaze latched on to the distant entrance to the restrooms. She hadn't hidden out in a restroom since her early, awkward teenage years, but the thought of doing so at this instant was infinitely tempting. But, she took a deep breath. Logan was watching her, testing her, seeing how far he could push her and she wasn't going to give him the satisfaction of running away. She looked over her shoulder at him. "You're certainly impossible to ignore." Her comment could be interpreted as a compliment...or not.

Her deliberately ambiguous response seemed to please him because he smiled. A smile that crinkled the skin around his eyes. She found herself smiling back and holding his gaze for the longest time, losing herself in the depths that were as tempting and sinful as chocolate. There was something so different, so...invigorating in the way he teased her, and the way he allowed and encouraged her to tease him back.

Eduardo cleared his throat. "How are the leBlanc negotiations coming along?"

Logan's smile vanished and he swung his gaze to Eduardo. "I never discuss business when I'm on a date with a beautiful woman."

"Of course not," Eduardo said, something smug and unattractive in his eyes. "And I'm interrupting." With a small bow he excused himself.

Logan dropped his hand from her back.

Rebecca stepped a little away from him, needing more air, more space. "Shall we go back in? I don't know that I'm ready for more performances like that." She put her champagne flute on a passing waiter's tray.

"But you're a natural. If I didn't know better I would

have thought there was real warmth, almost heat, in that gaze."

Rebecca lifted her chin. "Then it's a good thing you do know better." His laughter was quiet and deep as he offered her his arm and they began walking. Beneath her palm she felt the solid strength of a powerful forearm.

"What's Eduardo's interest in leBlanc?"

She lifted a shoulder. "Probably his new stepfather."

"Who is…?"

They reached their seats and she slid her hand from his arm. "Theo Summerfield."

"Damn."

"That's a problem?"

"No. But I should have known. I hadn't made the connection." He stood while he waited for her to sit in one of the plush red seats then lowered himself beside her.

"Theo is Eduardo's mother's fourth husband. And Eduardo is the son of her second. It's not easy to keep track of."

"No. But it's the sort of thing I do like to keep track of."

"Know your opposition?"

"Exactly. For instance, I did know that you and pretty boy—"

"Eduardo."

"That you and Eduardo were once an item."

He knew her dating history? Not that it required extensive research or even a particularly good memory. In stark contrast to what she knew of him, her list of suitors was short. "Not an item. We went out. Twice." She really should have learned after the first time. All Eduardo had wanted was the kudos for dating a princess. He still did. He had political aspirations. And from what she knew, his stepfather was currently in the process of seeking "By

Royal Appointment" endorsement for his line of breakfast foods. He too wanted her to date Eduardo.

"It's beginning to make sense," Logan said.

"What is?"

"The 'once a day and for five seconds only' rule you have."

She wanted to disagree with him but maybe he was right. The rules she'd tried to establish with Logan had been based on her previous—limited—experience. She'd only dated men who didn't push boundaries, who respected—too much—her position, failing to see who she was inside. Men who neither tempted nor taunted her.

But the thought that Logan had *researched* her was disconcerting on several levels. "Does this interest you appear to have in my social life mean you see me as the opposition?"

He leaned closer. "No. Not the opposition. But I make a point of knowing how things stand with the people I'm... dealing with. We're allies now, remember."

"Now, yes. Uneasy allies, I might add."

He shrugged and slipped his arm behind her shoulders, the fabric of his suit brushing against her skin. "But allies nonetheless. And I'm starting to think things might not always be uneasy. That in fact, some things might be very easy and enjoyable."

"That's right. The things that don't require us to talk. As I recall I'm allowed to sit next to you and whisper in your ear at the rowing regatta."

"There are other things that wouldn't require us to talk." His thumb moved slowly over her shoulder.

And the heat she'd thought she'd tamped down...stirred. "This is all some kind of game to you, isn't it? Like chess and you see me as a pawn."

"That's one way of looking at it. But I'd have to see you as the queen, don't you think? Do you play?"

"Not if I can avoid it. Chess is more Adam's game. I used to play with him but I didn't look far enough ahead and kept falling into the traps he'd set." The stray notes of the string section of the orchestra retuning violins and cellos sounded. "Do you play?" Did he set traps? Was she walking unwittingly into one?

"Occasionally. It's not really my thing, either. Takes too long."

"You played with your brothers?"

He nodded, offering nothing further. For some reason his upbringing, his brothers and the relationship they had intrigued her. Probably because she knew it would be so utterly different from her own experience of family life—brought up in a castle, largely by nannies and then a private all-girls school. The lights dimmed and the curtain rose.

"What about your parents?" He'd mentioned brothers several times but never a mother or father.

"Shh. It's starting."

"And you don't want to miss a thing?"

His lips stretched into a grin as he slid a little lower in his seat.

"What are you doing?"

"Getting comfortable."

The delicate strains of flute music twirled through the theater. "Don't you dare fall asleep," she said quietly.

"I wouldn't dream of it."

"You might not dream of it but you might actually do it."

He smiled, a glimpse of white teeth. "Help me stay awake then."

"What do you want me to do?"

"Too innocent." His smile widened as he raised an eyebrow and his gaze dipped to her legs, and the glimpse of thigh revealed by her dress.

Rebecca tugged her dress down a little. "Be serious."

"I was. I'll be fine. Just hold my hand."

As the dancers pirouetted onto the stage she slipped her hand into the one he held out for her, too enamored as always by that simple touch, so different than any other.

Logan drove back to the palace in silence. Floodlit gravel crunched beneath the wheels as he pulled to a stop in front of a discreet entrance to the towering west wing. Discreet it might be—but only in comparison to the main entrance. The armed, uniformed guards at the door were a whole new spin on Daddy waiting up in the porch rocker with a shotgun across his lap. Daddy might not be here in person but his eyes and ears and his firepower were. Logan grinned. He'd had his share of encounters with protective daddies. None quite of the caliber of Rebecca's father, though. But he'd never been one to back down in the face of a challenge.

Making sure the doors were locked—he didn't want an enthusiastic valet, or overly suspicious guard interrupting—he turned to her. Read and relished the uncertainty in her eyes. It didn't take a genius to figure out that she may not have had the same level of experience as he did. Conflicting urges surprised him. The urge to protect her vied with the urge to show her a world he suspected she knew little about, to show her things about herself she might not even know. And, of course, there was the urge to explore further what they'd begun on the steps of the plane.

She averted her gaze. "Thank you."

"Thank you?" So polite. So royal. So challenging. Logan slid his hand behind her neck. Lustrous hair caressed the back of his hand, silky skin lay beneath his fingers. A world of sensation at his fingertips.

If they had, as she'd suggested, taken a royal car they would have had the entire drive back and the entire comfortable width of the Bentley's backseat.

She glanced at him but then looked back out the windshield, her delicate throat moving as she swallowed. "For coming to the ballet. I know it wasn't—"

He did what he'd wanted to do the entire drive home, the entire evening actually, since the moment he'd first seen her in that dress. He dropped his other hand, slipped it through the split in her gown, the split that had worked its way to midthigh. He touched sleek skin only a little above her knee and still had to suppress his groan even as he enjoyed her breathless gasp.

She turned to him, her eyes wide with surprise and something more. Curiosity? Temptation?

She opened her mouth and he covered her lips with his before she could say anything. Captured her words, her breath. She was too full of questions and protests and analysis. Too reluctant to trust in the obvious. The simple. And the obvious and the simple were the heat that flamed right here and right now as his tongue found and teased hers. As he felt her tentative return exploration. Not just her tongue but the hand that snaked around his neck, pulling him closer, threading into his hair.

Kissing her was like kissing a dream, effortless perfection, no awareness of anything other than their simple joining and sharing, mouths that fit as though made only for each other. She sighed into him, deepening the kiss. Drugging him with her taste, her scent.

They had something.

Something far more potent than he'd even thought to consider.

She was far more potent to him than he'd thought to consider. He, who liked to think through all the possible scenarios, had bought in to the carefully constructed portrayal of her as someone without spontaneity, without passion. The Ice Princess.

How wrong he'd been.

The Ice Princess currently had him heading toward fever point. And it wasn't just him. She moved beneath him, arching and pressing. Her body soft and yielding against his and yet straining to get closer. Her mouth beneath his, supple and seeking, her leg beneath his palm, moving ever so slightly away from the other, inviting access. Another gasp escaped her as he slid his hand farther up the soft skin, his thumb finding the thin silken barrier, pressing against it. He wanted it all—her surprise, her passion. The taste of her, the feel of her. Only after lifting her hips to press against him in return did she seem to realize what she was doing. Her legs snapped back together, trapping his hand in the velvet warmth between them in an exquisite prison.

Logan lifted his head. The shock and desire in her parted lips and in her wide eyes reflected his own.

Who knew?

He lifted a corner of his mouth in as much of a smile as he could manage right now. While his heart still pounded and blood still rushed in his veins.

"How did you do that?" she whispered.

"That wasn't me, sweetheart, that was you." He curved his palm where it lay blissfully snared against her thigh. Then, regretting the necessity, he withdrew it.

"No."

He nodded.

"No." She refused to believe. "That was you. It had to be. Because if it was me it would have…"

"Would have what?"

"Happened before," she said with a confused frown. "I have to go." She reached for the door handle.

"Leave it. I'll get your door." He couldn't tell her that the plunge into the conflagration that just touching his lips to hers had caused was new and different for him, too. He'd been there before. But not like this, blindsided by the chemistry, insensible to anything else.

"It's okay." She raised her hand. About to signal a doorman? "One of the—"

"I'll get it." He cut her off. "It's what I do when I bring a woman home from a date."

"Oh."

Though she was like no other woman and this was like no date he'd ever been on before. He was out and walking around the front of the car before she could change her mind. Opening her door he reached for her. She didn't take his hand. "Afraid of me, Princess?"

She straightened to her full height. Even in her heels she was only somewhere between his chin and his nose. But somehow she managed to look down her nose. "Yes, Logan. I think I am." A gentle breeze swept a tendril of hair across her lips. She reached for it before he could and tucked it behind her ear, denying him that excuse of touching her further.

Her candor surprised him. He'd expected her to bluff her way out with royal composure. Not to admit that she was unsettled. Afraid of him. He reached for the hands she'd kept from him. "Don't be." Soon they would be someplace where they had time to explore what sizzled between them. Where he had time to explore *her*.

"I don't see how I can't be. That..." She inclined her head toward the car, the jerky movement a far cry from her normal gracefulness. "That. You. What happened. The way I forgot about everything."

"That's what's supposed to happen when you kiss someone." Admittedly it didn't always. And almost never so completely and so quickly.

"In books."

"In life." There was a faint tremor to the hands he held. Again the conflict. Soothe away the tremors or make her tremble all over? For him.

"Not to me."

"Ever?"

She shook her head. Her eyelids dropped, shielding her gaze. In the distance the tower clock chimed.

That it hadn't happened before, but had happened with him, pleased him inordinately.

"I stay in control. It's who I am. It's everything." She said the words with a vehemence that was perhaps meant to convince herself as well as him.

He waited until she looked back at him, caught and held her gaze. So serious, so wary. "I can respect that. I like control, too. But there are times when it's overrated and times when it's just plain wrong." He dropped his voice. "Like when making love." Her eyelids lowered. And he knew that, like him, she, too, was imagining what that might be like between them. He'd never expected things to get this far this fast between them, like fireworks bursting into life at the touch of a match, flaming gloriously, belying a simple exterior.

She took a step back from him, gave a small shake to her head, but tellingly left her hands in his and her eyes on his face—searching for something. Confirmation, reassurance, promise? He didn't know which or how much of any he could give her. He just knew that against reason and judgment he wanted—almost desperately—to make love with her. And when they did there would be nothing controlled about it.

Dropping one hand, he led her to her door and she turned to him. "Good night." She was struggling to put back in place the barriers they'd broken through tonight. She might not know it but they were broken for good. Some fences couldn't be mended.

"Good night? You're not inviting me in?" He kept his tone light, teasing. He didn't want to frighten her with the sudden intensity of his desire for her, and he didn't want her to realize his weakness for her. She still had some figuring out to do. For that matter, if he was sensible, so did he.

The crown prince's warning and his concerns for his daughter rang in Logan's ears. If they took this further the potential for hurt grew exponentially. And the last thing he wanted to do was hurt her.

"No." Her eyes darted to the various staff standing discreet distances away, and doing their best to appear invisible. "It wouldn't be appropriate."

He leaned in and brushed his lips over hers. Kissed her jaw once. Then whispered in her ear, even as he inhaled one last breath of her scent and spoke on impulse, "No. I'd make sure it was anything but appropriate."

Six

Rebecca finally had it figured out by the time she finished her shower the next morning. She ought to have—she'd spent enough hours tossing and turning through the night thinking of Logan and their…situation. His kisses and what they did to her. She dried herself off, hopping as she patted the towel beneath her foot. He was so unlike any other man she'd known that he kept her off balance.

Planting her feet firmly on the cool marble she looked sternly in the mirror, willing conviction and strength into her expression. Sometimes you just had to look like you were in control to convince other people you were and even to believe it yourself. It wasn't, however, a strategy that was working today.

Because of the unpredictable impact Logan had on her thought processes, on her senses and even on her body, she would have to keep him at a distance emotionally. Which shouldn't be too hard because he didn't strike her as the sort to encourage deep emotions.

She dropped the towel and reached for the body lotion. In their remaining weeks together, an insistent voice whispered, maybe he could teach her...things, show her...things. Things that weren't deep and meaningful or emotional, but things that were shallow and physical. Things no one had ever thought to show a princess and things a princess had never thought, or dared to ask. They would have their scheduled dates and there would be private moments.

Like last night.

She could ask him to...tutor her.

She smoothed the scented lotion on her legs and remembered the touch of Logan's palm on her thigh in the darkness. Gently abrasive and fiercely seductive. Banishing the recollection she pulled silk underwear on—and was reminded again.

She caught her reflection, the uncertainty on her face, in the full-length mirror. She turned to the side, stood straighter. It was a long time since she'd really looked at herself. She wasn't tall and willowy like the model girlfriends her brother dated or the type of women Logan had gravitated toward when she'd watched him socially. But there was nothing overtly wrong with her, nothing that makeup and well-tailored clothes couldn't compensate for. And she had to hope that within the confines of their agreement, what she could offer him in return was enough.

She pulled her hair back into a ponytail and examined the effect. Maybe she could pretend for a time to be normal, to be the type of woman a man like him, who, despite phenomenal financial success, still enjoyed life's simple pleasures, might go out with.

Because clearly the woman she actually was, a princess

whose life was governed by rules and protocol, was not that type of woman.

She tried to imagine herself in jeans and a T-shirt.

She'd always been curious about what life outside the confines of her role might be like. Logan, more than any other man she knew, could give her a taste of that. If in doing so she kept her father's matchmaking at bay and helped Logan achieve what he wanted in San Philippe, then it was, as he'd called it, a win-win situation.

Her phone rang. Logan's number showed on the screen. As if she'd conjured him. Had he been thinking of her?

"I need to see you again," he said when she answered. "Soon."

Her heart gave a girlish flutter at his use of the word *need*. Ridiculous. She wasn't a teenager. She was supposed to be mature and dignified. At all times. Rebecca looked away from the bright hope in her reflection. Away from the fact that she wore only her underwear while she was speaking to him. A concept that seemed almost scandalous and, well, just a little bit exciting. As were his words.

"We could go out to dinner tonight," she suggested.

"It needs to be something your father will be present at."

The glimmering bubble of delusion burst. Rebecca turned away from the mirror. "Ah."

"I have an unscheduled meeting with leBlanc Industries next week. And one of the members of the board of directors and the main opponent to leBlanc signing with me will be there. He's an ardent royalist believing firmly in tradition and connections. If I've been seen with you *and* your father, it'll help my cause."

She was a means to an end for Logan. She had to remember that. This was business for him. "He's careful about being seen to sanction individuals."

"But he'd do it for you?"

"He might, yes." He would if she asked.

"I'm not asking for an audience with him, just to be seen with you, at something he's at."

This was their agreement. Rebecca pushed aside her disappointment and mentally sifted through what she could remember of her schedule, specifically events at which her father would also be present. "There's not much coming up that you could attend."

"I don't care what it is. It just needs to be soon."

Walking through to her bedroom, she called up her schedule on her organizer. "There is one thing on this Thursday afternoon, and it's semipublic so my father won't be too concerned about you being there," she said hesitantly, "but I don't know that it's your kind of thing."

"Whatever it is. Count me in."

"Thank you. I think." Logan spoke the words through partially gritted teeth and Rebecca smiled.

He sat by her side under the white silk canopy shading the temporary stage. A "new rose" walk in the San Philippe botanical gardens was being dedicated today and each of the seven rose breeders who'd developed one of the feature roses in the walk had been invited to explain the genesis and naming of each flower. They were passionate about their craft and their blooms. And each one of them strove to outdo the others, to demonstrate his or her depth of skill and knowledge, part science, part art, part magic.

But all seven of them speaking, it was too much, even for her. Most of the guests did their best to look riveted but many were fidgeting. And those were just the ones Rebecca could see from her elevated position. Doubtless there were those fighting sleep in the back rows warmed by the sun and lulled by the speakers.

Which reminded her of Logan. Worried, she glanced at him. His eyes were open though a little glazed. Sensing her scrutiny, he leaned closer, his shoulder brushing against hers. His scent tempting, beguiling, making her want to close her eyes and inhale deeply. "What are you thinking about?" she asked.

"I was wondering how the Cubs will do this season."

Figured he wouldn't be contemplating the subtleties of rose breeding. Not that she blamed him. She'd like to see a baseball game one day. See what all the fuss was about. She imagined sitting next to Logan at a game as opposed to the opening of a rose walk, and didn't need any special knowledge to know it would be an entirely different experience, *he* would be a different man. Keyed up, sitting forward in his seat. "If it keeps you from snoring I guess it's a good thing."

"What do you think about, Princess, when you're trying to look interested in something that holds no interest for you? What are you thinking about now?"

Him. His shoulder so close to hers. His jaw, strong and masculine. "I try to find something of interest in what I'm supposed to be doing. It's usually possible." Usually. But not always. Occasionally the distractions were too great.

He nodded toward the podium. "I take it there would have been bloodshed if just one of the esteemed rose breeders had been given the privilege of addressing a royal audience."

"You have no idea."

"Isn't it taking political correctness a little too far?"

"This is nothing," she said quietly. "The royal secretaries devote significant portions of their days, their lives even, to making sure people are treated evenly. That no one is seen to receive undue favor without warrant, and that those who warrant it are given it."

The scent of roses drifted on the warm breeze. The third speaker was an internationally respected expert but he was no orator, his voice an unfortunate monotone.

"It's a challenge, isn't it? One of those impossible fairy-tale tasks set by kings in order that no one actually be able to win the hand of his daughter. Given the choice I'd rather brave the fire-breathing dragon. This one feels more like trying to drain the undrainable well."

"The worthy ones always managed it." As a young girl she'd daydreamed about her own knight in shining armor, someone who'd slay dragons for her or tirelessly drain the well.

Logan slid his sunglasses on and settled a little deeper into his seat. Speaking of daydreams… She leaned closer, caught a hint of his scent, far more tempting than that of roses. "Do not go to sleep again. It's broad daylight."

He tapped the side of the sunglasses. "No one will be able to tell."

Maybe he was teasing her; after all, this was supposed to be important to him. The trouble with Logan was that she couldn't be sure. She nudged him with her elbow, hoping the movement was subtle enough to avoid detection by anyone watching. "It'll be over soon."

"Not soon enough. Are you a patron of the rose breeders' association?" He settled lower still.

"No." She nudged a little more forcefully.

"Then it doesn't matter so much." He crossed his long legs in front of him at the ankles.

"It matters. It always matters."

He shook his head. "How do you do it, sit through these things so serenely? So…awake? Forty minutes and I'm more than ready to make a run for it."

"Coffee and training. Don't forget you insisted on attending. And trust me, if you fall asleep you'll definitely make the papers but not for the reasons you're wanting."

He sat a little straighter, but then shuddered as the speaker droned on. "How do you bear it?"

"It's my job."

"And you can't even quit."

No. She couldn't quit. Though the thought had never occurred to her. It was who she was. You couldn't quit being yourself. It left you purposeless. With no identity. Didn't it?

"We're definitely going to be doing something off my list next. The ballet and a rose garden back-to-back is too much like torture."

"You wanted this."

"I know. That makes it worse," he said with such feeling she almost felt sorry for him.

"Next is polo. That's yours."

"Better. Horses, competition, sweat, noise. It couldn't get much different."

"The rose breeders are fiercely competitive. There have been accusations of theft and sabotage in the past."

"Now, that would be more interesting." The speaker sat down to polite applause. Another stood. "How much longer will this go on?"

"It'll get faster now. The next few speakers aren't quite so fond of the sound of their own voices."

He stifled a yawn. "That woman in the front row, the one with the enormous hat."

Rebecca knew instantly who he was referring to. Her hat, smothered in apricot silk roses, was possibly the largest sun hat she had ever seen. And she'd seen a lot of hats. The two people seated on either side of her were leaning subtly outward to avoid hitting it. "Mrs. Smythe-

Robinson. She loves all things royal, knows more about us than I do even, and her second love is gardening."

"I thought maybe she was planning on making a run for it, that the hat was camouflage. You know, crouch down amongst the bushes and tiptoe for the exit."

Rebecca stifled her smile at the thought of the portly Mrs. Smythe-Robinson, a stickler for protocol, doing any such thing.

"But if she's not going to use it, I say we do. I'll create a diversion, you get the hat, it's big enough for both of us, and we make a run for it."

Laughter hiccupped within her. She oughtn't to be laughing. These things were not supposed to be funny. But it was such a change to be sitting with someone who didn't take them seriously and didn't even pretend to.

"I thought you needed to be seen with my father."

"Photographers snapped us arriving together. Your father's here. The right connections will be made." A slide show, set to orchestral music, began playing on the screen to the side. "What do you say? On three?" he asked.

She focused on her duties, her responsibilities—now was not the time to let him distract her. "There's a ribbon to cut."

He sagged back into his seat. "The ribbon cutting is your job, I take it?"

She nodded. "It's a hereditary role." And she didn't need to ask how insignificant that would look to someone who ran a multinational corporation he'd founded after dropping out of college. "I took over after my mother died." The mother whose grace and warmth had added elegance to whatever she did. The mother who'd died when Rebecca was a child.

His hand closed around hers. Was that sympathy? "So

you're pretty handy with knives and scissors," he said half a minute later.

"Just some of my many talents. Timing is very important."

"Don't belittle your skills or responsibilities. I know you work with schools and hospitals and that both the local fashion and tourist industries credit you with their recent upsurges in business, and that The Princess Foundation has raised a huge amount of money to benefit many charities."

"I do my job."

"You do. And you do it well. And I owe you an apology."

"An apology?" She smiled. "That's not a word I'd have thought would often pass your lips."

He matched that smile, his own wry. "It's not. Because I try never to be in the wrong. And generally I'm successful. But I came here with preconceived notions of royalty and I let them color my opinion of you. I even said as much to you. Which you took with remarkably good grace. Which made it all the worse as I came to realize how wrong I was. So, yes, I apologize."

"Thank you." What else could she say?

"There's that good grace again. The one that almost makes me feel worse. You could try gloating?"

"Gloating's not really my style."

"I've noticed. It's one of the many things I admire about you."

"Are you up to something? Is there an agenda here I'm not seeing?"

Logan laughed. "Not at all. It's just…you're different from any other woman I've known. And I have to admit I like those differences. The whole serenity thing you have going…it's nice to be around. Very tranquil. I don't have a lot of tranquility in my life."

"So tranquil you fall asleep?"

His smile flickered. "That wasn't a reflection on the company. What I meant was that when I'm with you the things that drive me ease. They just don't seem quite so important. It's almost a relief."

"I'll add that to my list of skills."

"There are other skills and talents I'd like to explore further," he said a few moments later. The hand around hers tightened. His thumb stroked. Now that he'd given up fantasies of escape apparently he'd turned to other fantasies, other ways of disconcerting her.

The innuendo was clear. But she had no *other* talents. Not of the sort she thought he was referring to. But perhaps she could learn. As she looked away she became aware that the press photographers were paying at least as much attention to Logan and her as they were to the man at the podium. She smiled at him, hiding her uncertainty, and then returned her gaze to the speaker. Though she kept part of her attention on Logan, aware of his hand, aware of the potential for him to drift to sleep. And wondering whether she had the nerve to put the exhilarating idea still percolating in her head to him.

He, she was certain, was more than talented.

Twenty minutes later she'd cut the ribbon—precisely—and the guests were finally permitted to stroll the new walk. The small crowd stood with an enthusiasm that owed as much to being allowed out of seats that had become progressively more uncomfortable as it did to the desire to see and smell and enjoy the blooms and the walk. And, of course, to be seen in return.

As she and Logan meandered the cobbled path, he maneuvered them so that they fell a little behind the main group clustered around her father and the rose breeders. They strolled up a gentle rise and paused. Not too far away a lake glittered, and several small rowboats wended their way across its surface. "It looks so serene," Rebecca murmured. "I watch the boats every time I come here."

"Ever been in them?"

"No. It's not really the thing."

"The thing?"

"The right look."

"But you'd like to?"

"Maybe. I've never rowed a boat. It looks fun."

Mrs. Smythe-Robinson detached herself from the main group and puffed back up the path toward them. "Speaking of fire-breathing dragons," Logan whispered.

As she approached, the older woman pointed to a rose-bush covered in apricot blooms. "This is the one Spriggs developed. I'm not sure it's his best."

"The floribunda," Logan said with creditable enthusiasm.

Rebecca hid her surprise. He'd been listening?

"No, no. It's a grandiflora."

"You're right, of course." He deferred politely to her.

Mrs. Smythe-Robinson smiled, set her sights on someone else and bustled away. Rebecca and Logan walked on. "Was she right?"

"Not according to what Spriggs himself said less than half an hour ago," Logan said.

"Very diplomatic of you."

"She didn't look like the type of woman I'd want to argue with. No chance of winning regardless of the rights and wrongs. And with some people even when you win you lose."

"You know who she is?"

"As it happens, yes. Her husband heads the government committee on foreign investment in San Philippe."

"And won't you need that committee's approval?"

"I already have that committee's approval. But she still didn't look like the type of woman I'd want to argue with."

"There's a type?" She pulled away from him on the pretext of smelling a luscious cream bloom. In reality she needed distance so that she didn't lean in instead.

"Most aren't worth the effort."

She looked up from the bloom. "Shall I take that as a compliment because you have no problem arguing with me?"

He offered his arm and she slid her hand over it. "Yes. But arguing with you has other benefits. I like seeing you get heated up, you make this indignant little huff. It's discreet, and kind of cute, but still a huff." He placed his hand over hers, holding it in place.

"I do not." She tugged at the hand but it was clamped against unrelenting muscle.

"See. Just like that one. And there's a most entrancing lift to your breasts when you do it."

"I did not huff." She kept her voice calm despite wanting to grit her teeth. "And even if I did, you shouldn't be looking at my breasts."

"I've tried not to. Believe me, I've tried. But like I said, they're entrancing. And I like seeing the conflict within you, the repressed passions. Even when you sound calm, like now, your eyes give you away. They flash silvery fire. A fire that could be better directed. A fire that must be all-consuming when you make love."

She did her best to hide the reaction he so clearly watched and waited for. It wasn't easy. Curiosity about what making love with him would be like flared. And Logan talking about making love, here, was too much.

"Enough." Finally she freed her hand. Now she just needed to wrest control of the conversation back. "You've had your fun but you can't say that type of thing here. No matter how bored you are." Because he was entertaining himself at her expense. She was sure of it.

Logan guided them down another narrow side path farther away from the small crowd.

She spoke quietly. "One of the things you need to learn about royal—"

With a hand on her shoulder he turned her to face him and covered her lips with his and what she'd been about to say fled her mind. Her awareness slid into the sudden vortex of sensation, the feel of his lips against hers, soft and warm and seeking, his hands on her shoulders anchoring her close to the hard strength of his body. He'd been talking about making love and now his lips were on hers and her traitorous body primed by his earlier words and the images he'd sown leaped in response as his tongue teased. His grip on her tightened, something in this kiss changed, heat flared. And that quickly she knew there was nothing academic about her desire for him to tutor her. It was all physical. A compulsion that sprang from the repressed passions he'd alluded to.

Her sun hat tumbled to the ground. And still it was several seconds before Logan broke the kiss and stepped back. His gaze darkened, then he blinked and bent to sweep up her hat, giving Rebecca precious seconds to regroup before he was again looking at her. "You were saying?" he asked.

She could read nothing in his gaze. Nothing of the confusion that assailed her. Nothing of the arousal that flooded her. She bit her lip. Hard. "Why did you do that?" she asked, watching his lips, full of sensual promise.

"Stop so abruptly? Because we were at our five seconds." The lips quirked.

She was losing control. She had to focus. Not on his lips but on his words. She looked at his ear instead. "Not stop. Start. When I was in the middle of trying to say something to you." Darn it, he even had nice ears, curving ridges and hollows that invited touch.

"Because I thought it was going to be a lecture, and—" he winked "—because I can." How real was his nonchalance? The teasing light in his eyes that she'd grown accustomed to wasn't there. And there'd been something far from nonchalant in the kiss. But she had so little to compare it to, and was far from trusting herself to interpret Logan's state of mind. "It's been the best part of the day so far," he said easily.

"Oh." Had it? Would that it had anything like the impact on him that it did on her. She knew she'd relive it later tonight. Maybe then she'd be able to sort out what it had meant to her.

Liar, a little voice whispered. The kiss had, without a doubt, been the best part of her day, too. And it had promised so much more. A promise that called to her, pulled at her. Logan was a window of opportunity. A window to another world.

He glanced ahead to where the approved press photographers lurked. "And it'll make a nice shot for the papers. We may as well give them something they can use, something that works for us, otherwise they'll find something of their own that may not suit our purposes so well."

"Like you yawning?"

"Precisely."

It was all about his plan, his goals, nothing more. He was so much more focused than she was. So much more in control. But perhaps that was a good—safe—thing. "Warn me next time."

"Why?"

"So I can be ready." So she didn't melt unthinkingly into his arms.

He appeared to give her request some thought then shook his head. "I prefer the element of surprise. I like the way you're kissing me back before you even realize what you're doing."

He was standing so close still. She ought to step away. Ought to, but connection, or maybe fear, or maybe desire, held her there. She wouldn't examine which.

"Besides," he said, "I was completely within the rules. Less than five seconds. And there haven't been any others today."

Rules. Rules and plans and appearances. How real was anything they shared?

He lifted her hat, placed it on her head, studied her for a second and then adjusted the angle so it was more to his liking. His arms framed her face, creating a strange intimacy between them, shutting out the rest of the world. She was about to thank him, politely, when he swooped in and planted another kiss on her lips—quick but gentle. "Technically that one may have been outside of the rules." He stepped back, took her hand and they started walking.

If no real sentiment was engaged didn't that mean her own secret plan was even more viable?

Thoughts and possibilities pursued her. For five minutes they walked in silence. All her life she'd been schooled in how to comport herself in public. But she'd had no guidance in private matters.

A father and two brothers had been a great help in all things royal. But that was where their help ended. Hearts and hormones weren't discussed—at least not in front of

GET FREE BOOKS and FREE GIFTS
WHEN YOU PLAY THE...

777

Just scratch off the silver box with a coin. Then check below to see the gifts you get!

SLOT MACHINE GAME!
YES!
I have scratched off the silver box. Please send me the 2 free Harlequin® Desire® books and 2 free gifts for which I qualify. I understand I am under no obligation to purchase any books, as explained on the back of this card.

225/326 HDL FEFC

FIRST NAME   LAST NAME

ADDRESS

APT.#   CITY

STATE/PROV.   ZIP/POSTAL CODE

7 7 7	**Worth TWO FREE BOOKS plus 2 FREE Mystery Gifts!**
🍒🍒🍒	**Worth TWO FREE BOOKS!**
♣♣♣	**Worth ONE FREE BOOK!**
🔔🔔🍒	**TRY AGAIN!**

Visit us at: www.ReaderService.com

H-D-07/11

The Reader Service—Here's How It Works:

her. She'd become good friends with Rafe's wife, Lexie. But it was still a relatively new friendship. Not the sort of deep sisterly connection she hoped they'd one day share.

No, any next step into the unknown was hers alone.

Could she ask Logan for more? Ask for an amendment to their agreement. A special clause. Because she wanted to know so much more. And Logan was the one who could teach her. He certainly had the…skills, and he wasn't from here, wouldn't be staying here. "Do you…"

"Do I what?"

"Do you…like…kissing me?" It wasn't the question she'd been going to ask, but it would lead her to the answer she sought without revealing too much of her vulnerability.

His eyes narrowed, as though suspecting some kind of trap. "Far too much."

"It's not just for the press?"

He shrugged. "It's for the press and for the public. But remember what we said about how we didn't need to pretend to enjoy a meal if it was a good meal?"

Yes, she did. So he enjoyed kissing her? As much as she enjoyed kissing him? Though she wasn't entirely sure that *enjoy* was the right word, it was too uncomplicated, too tame almost. Kissing him thrilled her, confused her, made her want…more, made her uncertain of herself even as it gave her pleasure. So many things, too much for something as uncomplicated as enjoyment. But still he was only kissing her because of their arrangement. He didn't need or want anything further from her than the appearance that they were in a relationship. That could work in her favor.

"I get to kiss you and enjoy it. Like tasting a delicacy that has you craving more. A definite win-win situation."

Somehow his words stirred an element of loss, too. She couldn't quite identify it. Somewhere along the line this had become something far more important to her than it ought to be. Not just showing her father that she was a woman capable of making her own decisions and controlling her life. But about showing herself that she was a woman. Not a princess.

Logan reached for a delicate dusky pink bloom, ran a blunt fingertip between the petals. "Do you know what these velvet petals make me think of?" Still teasing, still trying to disconcert her. He knew this type of conversation, this subtle flirtation, wasn't her forte.

"Stop it. It's a flower, nothing more." The rose breeders would slay her if they heard her say that.

"Or how I have visions of laying you down on a bed of rose petals?"

"Logan. Don't." How had their conversation taken such a sudden swerve? How did he so easily plant images in her mind, or bring to life the images that she'd already allowed to grow?

"Or what?"

"Or I'll call Mrs. Smythe-Robinson back over."

A honey bee landed on the rose, collected pollen. "We can talk fertilization with her. I'm sure she'll have an opinion on the subject."

Ahead of them there was a burst of laughter.

"Can I ask you something?"

"You can ask me anything you want and I'll answer, but only something you actually want the answer to, because I'll be honest."

She believed that much of him, but she pressed her lips together because her thoughts flashed back to last night and this morning.

"Go on. One question. Anything. I dare you."

Ah, the Buchanan dare, she could hear the cockiness in

his voice, the expectation that nothing she could ask would throw him. "What if I asked you to…"

Her request faltered beneath the sudden intensity of his gaze. It was so easy to say things in her head. *Teach me pleasure. Teach me how to be myself when I'm with a man. Teach me what men like.*

"Go on." He couldn't possibly know what she'd been about to ask but there was a sudden wariness to his tone as though he at least knew it wasn't going to be a flippant request. Although maybe she could phrase it that way. *Teach me how to make pancakes for breakfast for the man I've just spent the night with.*

"Teach me—"

Those liquid brown eyes held her still, urged her on.

"Your Highness, there you are. We thought we'd lost you." Mrs. Smythe-Robinson bustled toward them, her program for the day's events in her hand, a small posse of enthusiasts behind her. "Can you can settle something for us? Was your mother's favorite color apricot or lavender?"

Relief washed through her at the interruption because she'd been suddenly afraid of Logan's response. He wanted her on his arm in pictures to further his company's goals. He had no need or desire to help her learn what she wanted to know. He had scores of willing women who needed no teaching whatsoever. She allowed herself to be drawn into settling the supposed debate.

Once, when looking at a child's artwork, her mother had exclaimed that the apricot crayon used was her favorite color. From that moment on she had been deluged with apricot-colored gifts. She had confessed to her family, but to no one else, that her favorite color was in fact blue. It had been a lesson for her mother, who had only been trying to be diplomatic. A lesson she had ample time over the following years to contemplate.

One of her father's secretaries approached her. "You're needed for the photos, ma'am."

She turned to Logan, realized that at least now with her question rightfully repressed she could look him in his lovely brown eyes. "This may take a while. And then I have to go straight on to a meeting of The Princess Foundation. I'll see you for the polo match tomorrow."

"Your question?"

"It doesn't matter now." She was hardly going to ask it with royal staff standing nearby no matter how much they pretended not to be listening.

He reached for her wrist before she could turn away, anchoring her to the spot. Heat snaked up her arm, slithered deep inside her. He held her gaze, his eyes serious, and gave a single slow nod. "Yes. I'll teach you."

Seven

Rebecca sat in the car given to her for the evening by the chief of security. It wasn't one she'd driven before. And never before had she sat so uncertain for so long.

Out of a desire to preserve the architectural heritage of San Philippe, there were no true high-rises in the city. So it was easy enough to look up at Logan's riverfront penthouse apartment.

But what if Logan's *yes* hadn't actually been in response to the question she'd wanted to, but hadn't quite asked? What if his *yes* had been "yes, I'll teach you to row a boat." He hadn't called her or made any attempt to contact her to discuss her question. Admittedly, it had only been a matter of hours since she'd asked it but if she didn't act now she'd lose her nerve. His windows revealed nothing. All she could make out was that lights were on inside. She looked from those uninformative windows to the phone clutched in her hand.

Spineless. Time to either go through with her plan or go home.

Men were supposed to like the hunt, the thrill of the chase. She knew that much. Desperate women who threw themselves at men were *desperately* unappealing. Then again, she didn't need Logan to like her, she just needed him to...help her.

On the ancient bridge spanning the river, couples walked hand in hand. Women leaned heads on partners' shoulders, so trusting, so gently intimate. Two looking almost as one. And here she was sitting alone in her car.

Following the photo session and then the meeting, her father had wanted a private conversation with her this evening. But she'd figured she'd face an inquisition over Logan so she'd cried off, explaining she'd already arranged to see Logan, knowing that her father would be in Switzerland for the next couple of days. She was becoming quite adept at evasion, at telling...things that weren't quite the truth. In her head she could almost hear Logan challenging her to call it what it was—a lie.

The only person she was practiced at lying to was herself. For so long she'd pretended she didn't have wants and needs of her own. In the time she'd known Logan he had made her far too conscious of her self-deceit. And more than anything else he made her conscious of those wants and needs.

She lifted her phone then closed her eyes and doubt flooded in.

She couldn't go through with it. What was she even doing here? What had she been thinking? She was not, and never would be, a normal woman. She'd never walked with her head resting on a man's shoulder. Because she couldn't depend on a man like that. She couldn't trust Logan—or any man—like that.

Because if you didn't trust someone they couldn't betray you. Trusting someone gave them power over you.

And Logan was too much an unknown quantity. Too unpredictable. Too uncontrollable. She had too much to lose.

A light rain began to fall, refracting the light on her windshield, obscuring the world outside, making it shimmer.

Home. She would go home where she was safe and knew the rules. They had a plan. A good plan. Safe, if not completely sensible. All she had to do was stick to it and pretend to date Logan for the allotted weeks. No more. No less.

The phone cradled in her palm vibrated and rang, making her jump. Logan's name lit up on the display. He needn't know anything. "Hello," she answered, keeping her voice casual, a little curious.

"What are you doing?" His voice was almost all curiosity. Curiosity with a hint of something knowing.

The knowing could only be her imagination, her guilt. "Reviewing the minutes from the foundation's meeting," she said with a bored sigh. But her lack of skill at lying shined through and she spoke a little too quickly, her voice a little too high.

"In your car?"

"Sorry?" She pretended she was confused, that she hadn't quite heard or understood a question that ought to make no sense. In part she *was* confused. He couldn't possibly know she was outside his apartment building. She looked around to make sure. There was no one near her car, no one paying any attention to it. The windows were darkly tinted.

"That is you, isn't it? Parked along the riverfront. Near the street lamp."

Her face heated in the darkness. Clearly he could, and did, know.

Part and parcel of being no good at lying was being no good at extricating herself from a lie. "I...I...have to go. I'll talk you later."

"You're sure you wouldn't rather see me sooner?"

"I have another call coming through. I think it's my father. Bye." She jabbed at the off button and let her head fall back against the headrest. But only for a few seconds while her heartbeat slowed. Anyone else in the world would surely have handled that better than she had. And she was a princess. She was supposed to be adept at handling delicate situations. Time to get a grip. She turned her key in the ignition and flicked on her lights. Illuminated in their beam, a tall, broad-shouldered man, his dark hair rumpled, walked toward her, his long, easy stride eating up the distance. Rebecca tapped her forehead against the steering wheel. She'd had extensive training in defensive, and evasive driving; hand-brake slides, high-speed escape maneuvers. But none of that would be any help to her now. There was no dignified retreat.

He tried her door. She pressed the button to unlock it and cut the engine. As he opened her door he held a hand toward her. She focused on that hand rather than his face and held on to it only until she stood. Eventually she had to look up. A frown creased his brow, not irritation but...concern? As his gaze traveled over her, assessing, the frown eased. His breathing was rapid but controlled. As though he had raced to get here? His button-down shirt was untucked and the first few buttons undone. He started walking and Rebecca had little choice but to fall into step beside him.

He asked no questions. She volunteered no explanation,

no excuses. Their footsteps sounded in quiet unison on the damp cobbles.

He walked slowly, strolling, when the part of her that wanted to escape her foolishness would have strode as though she could leave it behind. The more distance she put between her and her car, the more she could pretend she'd never parked on the road in front of his apartment, never been caught.

They crossed the pedestrian bridge that arched over the river. Balmy night air wrapped around them. Light shimmered and reflected in the inky water and on the damp cobbles. Ahead of them a couple walked hand in hand, their mingled laughter barely audible. And somewhere in the unseen distance the rapid, fluid notes of a Spanish guitar sounded.

Still she waited and mentally prepared for Logan's request for an explanation, or his mockery. She would be regal. She owed him no explanation. And she could rise above his mockery.

Neither came.

They just walked. Side by side. And she didn't feel regal. She realized, after maybe ten minutes, that this might be what it was like to feel normal. She could be with a man and not be compelled to make polite conversation. She could just…be, soaking in the sights and sounds and sensations.

His shoulder was close to her head. If she had the courage she'd reach for his hand, she could tilt her head, rest it on his shoulder like the couples she'd watched earlier. She did not have the courage. They passed beneath an ornate street lamp.

"Jeans?"

It was the last thing she'd expected him to ask. She'd

almost forgotten them. "I was trying to be normal. You know, not a princess. For an evening."

They walked on. His silence perplexing.

"What do you think? Of the jeans?" They both knew she could pretend but she could never be normal. Leopards and spots and all that.

"Nice." His hand swung back and patted her butt. "Very nice."

Nobody had ever patted her butt.

Rebecca smiled.

Logan lifted his arm and settled it around her shoulders, pulling her gently against him. And her head nestled against his shoulder as though designed to fit there. Sensation surged within her. She recognized it as happiness. Maybe she could walk like this all night long, circling the old parts of the city.

The sounds of the guitar grew clearer as they approached a strip of waterfront cafés and restaurants. "Have you eaten?" he asked.

"No." She'd escaped the palace rather than have dinner there.

"Neither have I." He steered her down a side road then stopped to open a door beneath a small green awning. "The view's not the same as on the waterfront, but it's quieter and the food—"

"Is divine?" she asked with a smile, remembering his previous descriptions of food.

He matched her smile. "It's simple but good. I think you'll like it."

They walked down a set of narrow stairs into the small restaurant redolent with aromas of Mediterranean cooking, olives and tomatoes and garlic. A short, balding man hurried up to them, arms held wide, his gaze and his smile lighting first on Logan, then freezing momentarily as he noticed Rebecca.

"Stefan," Logan said, "a quiet table, please."

"Of course." Stefan led them past the tables in the busy restaurant. The hum of conversation died away, to be replaced by whispers as diners realized who she was. Stefan showed them to a small corner table partially screened from the main restaurant. "I hope this will be suitable."

Stefan seated her. Logan sat opposite. A low candle flickered and danced between them.

She watched him, wondering when it was that Logan had changed from an irritant to the pearl.

Gradually the noise level resumed its initial volume.

Logan leaned back in his chair, watching her. And all the reasons this might not be such a great idea returned. The primary one being that now there was no escape for her, no avoiding his questions. Stefan placed a basket of assorted breads on their table. Rebecca smeared pesto on a small wedge of bread and waited. And waited. Until she could bear it no more. "I suppose you're wondering what I was doing outside your apartment."

"Actually, I was wondering what it must be like to have people fall silent just because you walk past them. To have people stare."

No one had ever asked her that. "It's just how it is, how it's always been. And it will undoubtedly help give you the profile you're after." She tried to keep the hint of hurt from her voice.

"Undoubtedly. So, you're here with me for my benefit?"

She didn't need the hint of sarcasm. "No. To be honest I'm not sure why I'm here with you. It seemed like a good idea to drive to your place. I know my father keeps tabs on me, that it will help convince him we have a real relationship. He has doubts."

"Smart man. And that was your only reason."

"And," she said and took a deep breath, "partly I just wanted to see you."

He hesitated for just a second. "And the other part?"

She waited while Stefan poured two glasses of ruby-red wine. But by the time he'd backed away her resolve was gone.

"The other part doesn't matter anymore."

"It always matters."

Rebecca took a sip of her wine. "Try this. It's divine."

And Logan laughed, recognizing her use of his own distraction techniques. She'd never met anyone whose laugh was quite so deep, quite so warming. It was one of the things, if not *the* thing, she liked best about him. There was such an appealing openness to his laugh, a complete lack of pretension. And it stirred a warmth within her, made her want him more. Made her wonder what it would be like to wake up to that smile, that laughter.

One of the other things she liked about him was his patience, though she knew that he could probably wield it as a weapon. He didn't press, seemed content to enjoy a meal that was as he'd predicted very good. She'd never heard of Stefan's, never eaten at a place like this in San Philippe. How much more was there for her to discover in her own small country?

She watched Logan's hands as he buttered bread, his lips as he sipped wine, the vitality in his eyes as he talked. Did he have anything like her level of awareness of him?

And she thought about those eyes watching her, those hands touching her, those lips kissing her.

Forbidden thoughts for a princess. She'd never before had trouble controlling her thoughts. It was what she did.

But Logan with his indifference to royalty made her keep wondering what it would be like not to be royal. Foolish notion. She couldn't, and wouldn't want to, change who she was. There was no point wondering.

No point in wondering, or wishing, for just a few weeks of anonymity. A few weeks when everything she said and did, or didn't say and do, wasn't scrutinized, reported, speculated on. A few weeks when she did something real. Her work with charities and schools and the arts was appreciated and did, she knew, benefit others. But sometimes she daydreamed about being a gardener, or a cook, or a painter—not an artist, but someone who painted walls and fences. Someone who at the end of the day could stand back and see what they'd achieved, other than neatly bisecting a ribbon or attending meetings.

And then she would berate herself for her daydreams because she knew that a good portion of the rest of the world daydreamed about having her life. She should be nothing but grateful.

"You have a very expressive face."

Rebecca's grip tightened on her fork. "Expressive?"

"Thoughts and emotions seem to flit through your eyes, even while you're looking far away."

"I do sometimes get a little caught up in my thoughts."

"A man could find it less than flattering."

As if he needed flattery from her. From anyone for that matter. "Doubtless women fawn all over you."

"Less, I expect, than men fawn over you."

"Actually, they don't. They tend to be intimidated."

"The threat of beheading, no doubt." It must be something to do with the candlelight, the way it glinted in his eyes.

Rebecca smiled. "No one's been beheaded in San Philippe in centuries."

"The dungeons?"

"They've been converted. Lighting. Heating. Part's even a gymnasium. You'd never guess their history." And despite her joking she knew it wasn't the nonexistent prospect of royal incarceration that kept suitors at bay. Though it was generous of Logan to give her that out. "No. I think I intimidate them." It was only men like Logan with an agenda—to make it into royal circles—who were prepared to overlook "her" and the glass bowl of her life in order to get what they sought. But at least Logan had been honest about that, which gave her leave to be honest in return.

"You're a princess. I can see how that might throw a man off his game, so to speak."

"But not you?"

"A person's a person. Regardless of what they do for a living, or where they live."

"Not so many people think like that. But it's more than the princess thing. I can be reserved." And sometimes she came across as remote, cold even. And the more uncertain she was the more reserved she became.

"I noticed," he said agreeably. "And haughty."

"No. Just reserved."

"Especially when you enunciate so clearly."

Like she just had. Years of elocution lessons were almost impossible to recover from. The princess persona was all of her training. All of her security. "Is it bad?"

"I was teasing you, Princess."

"That's another thing. I'm not always sure when people—and you in particular—are joking. And I don't want to not laugh if they've made a joke, but on the other hand I don't want to laugh if they weren't making a joke."

"I'm sure you're making this a whole lot harder than it

needs to be. How about you laugh if and when something strikes you as funny?"

She shook her head. "Too risky."

They lapsed into silence as their dessert arrived, a rich decadent chocolate tart, along with two spoons. The chocolate melted into her mouth, almost seeming to soak into it. They watched each other eat. Surreptitious glimpses and other more openly appreciative glances. And the liquid heat that she'd come to associate with Logan, as though her insides were following the example of the melting chocolate, filled her.

"Do you analyze everything?"

"Almost everything."

"Must be hell on your lovers."

Rebecca swallowed. "I wouldn't…I don't…analyze that. Only things about myself. Public things."

"I'm relieved to hear it."

Because? The question almost slipped out. Because he might think there was potential opportunity for her to analyze him, or merely because he believed in male solidarity?

He watched her over the rim of his wineglass, a frown clouding his expression. "There have been other lovers, haven't there?"

Relief, at the clarification—he did know what she'd asked of him, and had agreed to the same—warred with embarrassment at having this discussion here and now. For long seconds she looked at her wine, the red so dark it was almost black in the candlelight.

Then she looked up, met Logan's gaze. "Yes. But my experience is limited." He hadn't asked for numbers. "And I wasn't analyzing, not at the time, but I've come to think there might have been room for improvement."

One man, not much more than a boy really, at the end

of her first summer home from college. They'd met a few times over that week. It was a time she'd be happy to forget. It hadn't been, she suspected, earth-shattering for Ivan, either.

"It always gets better as lovers get to know one another's bodies."

She looked around the restaurant. "I'm not sure that this is a conversation we should be having here." No one was sitting close enough to hear, but all the same.

He nodded. "I just wanted to be clear."

"Would it have been a problem if there hadn't been others?" Why, when she was the one who didn't want to be having this conversation here and now, did stupid questions slip out? But she had no idea how men thought, not about things like this.

"Not a problem as such, but…" He shrugged.

How would it change things, she wanted to ask, but finally had the good sense not to.

Logan tipped his head back and looked for a moment at the ceiling. At the curving brickwork of what had once been some kind of cellar. He looked back at her. "Do you know how hard this is?"

"How hard what is?" she teased, quietly pleased with the flirtation and double entendre she was usually so appalling at.

She was rewarded with the flash of his grin. He leaned forward, resting his elbows on the small table. "How hard it is to sit here discussing this with you when from the very moment you asked me that question at the rose gardens, and if I'm honest from well before then, I've been imagining you naked and beneath me. How if we weren't in this restaurant I'd have hauled you against me and—" He looked back at the ceiling again, exhaling roughly.

His words thrilled her. She'd thought he was so in control.

Logan stood. "Let's go."

He took her hand and led her from the restaurant. They crossed back over the river to head in the direction of her car. And his apartment. There was still a voice, a royal cautionary voice, in the back of her mind insisting that she didn't know what she was doing. That she was making a mistake. It was the same voice that dictated her behavior day in and day out, year in and year out. That voice was saying run, get in her car and get out of here before she got into something she was ill-prepared for.

But the louder voice came from the hunger that stirred and swirled whenever she was with Logan, whenever she thought of him, the clamoring hunger that said this man could both inflame it and satisfy it.

This man who'd insinuated that she analyzed things too much.

She forced her mind to still, to focus on the here and now. They neared her car. "Thank you," she said. "I don't know when I've enjoyed a meal so much." It was true. The meal, eating with Logan, just being herself had been a rare pleasure. The sensual currents had heightened everything. A new and delicious experience.

"I could say the same. And although the food was good, it was the company that elevated it. You're an intriguing woman, Rebecca."

They were almost opposite her car when Logan paused in front of the wide, gold-lettered, glass doors of his apartment building, the oldest and most exclusive in San Philippe. He turned to her and lifted an eyebrow in inquiry.

And she knew what he was asking.

No discussion, no pressure, no expectation. That in

itself was a novelty. Her life was usually nothing but pressure and expectation. The decision was hers alone. She thought—hoped—that he had a preference as to her answer. He was, after all, issuing the invitation.

This was *the* moment. The fork in the road. And, for all her angst, it was a surprisingly easy decision. She wanted this. She wanted it academically for all sorts of reasons that made sense in her head but she wanted it physically, as a woman. She wanted it inside and out. And deeper still there was a yearning in her heart for this connection with Logan.

He held her gaze, his searching and utterly serious, as she nodded. In turn, Logan nodded to the doorman who opened the door and ushered them through. The sounds of the street outside were silenced as the door closed behind them.

Eight

Inside Logan's apartment, Rebecca crossed to the mullioned windows overlooking the street. Logan came to stand beside her, his shoulder a whisper away from hers, his scent subtle and warming. Down below, her car sat clearly visible on the far side of the road. Nothing covert about it. A nearby street lamp dimly illuminated the interior through the front windshield. She closed her eyes. She hated it when she was an idiot. He would have had little trouble identifying her. How long had he watched her before calling her?

"Give me your keys and I'll park your car in one of my spaces below the building."

"Oh. Thank you." She handed him the keys. Their fingers brushed. A small current of desire sped through her. He felt it, too—she saw it in his eyes. He closed his hand around the keys and strode toward the elevator.

She crossed to the couch to sit. And then, unable to sit

still, stood. She took the opportunity of his absence to look around his apartment. The sparse furnishings were at odds with the ornate interior and symbolic of a man passing through. The clean modern lines of the couch and single angular armchair contrasted with plaster moldings and a crystal chandelier and rich red velvet curtains. An acoustic guitar leaned against the couch. The instrument was the only personal touch in the whole room, the only thing that gave any clue as to its inhabitant. A low coffee table was pulled close to the couch. She could imagine Logan sitting on the couch, feet on the coffee table, guitar in his arms.

With him gone, the apartment was quiet and still and she had further opportunity to doubt the wisdom of her decision to come up here. She curled her hands into fists. It was the right decision and she would go through with it.

He would leave San Philippe once he had what he wanted. That was what made it—him—safe.

Rebecca was still staring at the battered instrument when he came back. She turned to see him standing on the far side of the living room watching her. "What sort of music do you play?"

"Whatever takes my fancy at the time."

"I'd like to hear you."

"Some other time, maybe."

It was nothing personal and she shouldn't take it that way. Some people didn't like playing for others. She looked back toward the view and the glittering city outside. This was all feeling too planned, too academic.

Warm fingers touched her jaw, turned her head. Her eyes met warm deep chocolate. A hint of a question lingered there along with a hint of intent. His lips were a serious, straight line. "Rebecca—"

She stepped in close, rose up on tiptoes and pressed her lips to his, needing to silence whatever he'd been going to say or ask. Yes, she knew what she was doing, she was sure. And yes, she most definitely did want this.

She felt his lips curve into a smile as his hands went to her shoulders and he pulled her closer still. His lips parted and moved with an assurance and pleasure her own lips had quickly come to recognize and her body had quickly come to respond to. Suddenly nothing felt planned or academic. There was only now, his lips on hers, his body against hers, his hands framing her face.

And there was no need for words or questions. But need aplenty for this. Just this connection.

Again no pressure, no expectation. In their stead, enjoyment, delight.

And heat.

He gave with his kiss. Gave of himself. Gave pleasure.

Sensation sang through her body as she let herself take. She wanted his touch and the taste of him. She wanted the wonder of his exploration, the delight of her own discovery.

Her hands found his chest, fingers splaying over powerful contours, relishing the warm silk over hard muscle. So male. So intriguing. So infinitely tempting. And beneath silk and muscle the beat of his heart. So human. She slid her hand beneath his shirt so that his skin all but scorched her palm where it came to rest on his chest. His heart seemed to beat right into her hand, as though if she curled her fingers she would be able to cradle it.

And all the while lips and tongue tasted and tempted, dared and challenged and invited.

She accepted the invitation, kissing him back, discovering the secrets of his mouth. Those lips that so often quirked in amusement were now hers for the taking and claiming hers in return. He angled his head, deepening his kiss. The hint of his beard gently abraded. There was something restrained in his kiss, she felt it and thought maybe she should be grateful for that. Maybe she was. But, then again, maybe she wasn't.

Her second hand joined the first, exploring the breadth of his torso, over sparse hair and small nipples, sliding around the hard strong back. Everything so male, so different. And everything feminine within her thrilled and leaped in response to what he was doing to her, to what she was doing to him and to the sensations possessing her.

She pressed harder against him, pressed her hips against his. She felt the shape of him.

A low masculine groan resonated somewhere between chest and throat and that sense of restraint she thought she'd felt shattered as the kiss became fiercer, hungrier.

He broke the kiss, bent and scooped her into his arms, striding through his apartment to his bedroom, setting her down gently on her feet beside an enormous bed.

Enough silver light from the city outside filtered through the windows to illuminate the angles of his face and a jaw set with determination, lips full and skilled in arts she knew little of but hungered to know more. His brow was etched with concentration as he worked at the small buttons that ran down the front of her blouse. When he had enough undone he pushed a shoulder of her blouse aside, pressed those lips to heated skin. Rebecca shuddered with savage delight.

He jerked his head upward and pulled back, and she knew a pang of loss caused by the distance. Had she done something wrong—responded too freely, not responded enough?

"I want you." He said the words he'd once said so clinically. This time his voice was a rough growl threaded with need. "Tell me," he said, "that this is what you want.

Tell me now." He gripped her shoulders, ready to either set her away or pull her closer. "I need to hear the words."

The raw edge to his voice thrilled her, his suave control was gone—for her. She lifted her hands to cup his jaw, tilted her head to meet the fierce expression in his eyes. "This is what I want," she said quietly. "You are what and who I want."

His Adam's apple moved in his throat. But that was his only movement. Her heart thumped as she waited at the brink of a precipice, not quite knowing how to force a leap from it. Why was he holding back? She knew he wanted this. It was there in his kisses, it was there in the rapid tattoo of his heart, the shallow breathing. She recognized the mirror of her desire.

"Think of it as a royal command." She kept her gaze on his as she dropped her hands to the remaining buttons of her blouse, picking up where he had left off. Then she tossed her blouse to the floor.

Those lips that so fascinated her quirked in a flicker of a smile. "I'm yours to command," he said as his head lowered to hers and as he eased a bra strap from her shoulder and kissed the spot where it had lain, then nipped her. And that quick gentle press of teeth on her skin arrowed need through her.

She knew with a fierce satisfaction that this moment, this thing between them was just that, something between the two of them alone. He was a man and she was a woman. Not a princess. Just a woman. Filled with a feminine power and feminine needs that only he could satisfy.

And then her bra was gone. Logan stepped back. Looked, admired, then lifted his hands to her breasts, rubbed thumbs over pebbled nipples. Her insides tightened with need for him, her legs almost gave way as she leaned in to his touch.

The imbalance in their dress seemed unfair. Rebecca reached out to undo his buttons, and pull his shirt off him.

And then she stilled.

His body, what she could see of it, which wasn't yet enough, was…beautiful. He had a broad sculpted chest with a light covering of hair, a lean hard abdomen. There, too, a faint trail of hair led her gaze downward to the snap on his jeans.

He stepped in, scooped her into his arms and set her gently on the bed. With tender haste he peeled what remained of her clothing from her as though unveiling a long-sought treasure. Raising her arms above her head, he anchored them there with one hand, trailing fingertips and kisses over her body—her face, her throat, breasts and arms, and each of her fingers. He explored as though he wanted to learn every inch of her. He pressed velvet soft kisses behind her knees, the soles of her feet, parts of her that should not be so sensitive but that were aflame at his touch. She writhed and rose up to meet him. And then he began the slow journey back up again.

And when he pressed his kisses between her thighs she could no longer keep her arms above her head, and instead plunged her fingers into the rich silk of his hair as her body jerked with the sensations that jolted through her.

Surely it was wrong to feel this intensely. Wrong and so wonderfully right. The rational part of her, hanging only by a thread, slipped away so that there was no thought, only exquisite pleasure. Her head thrashed with clamoring need for something she couldn't quite reach.

And then she reached it. Or rather it reached her, sweeping through her, wracking her body. She tried to suppress the cries of surprise and passion but they escaped.

And then Logan, broad shouldered and fierce, rose up above her. He sheathed himself and slid inside of her, the length of him stretching and filling her. So that where she'd thought it couldn't be possible to feel more, she felt so very much more.

They moved together, skin against skin, slowly, beautifully, moving as one, desire quickening, until they melded into a powerful, crashing rhythm, something desperate and primal. Until once again she cried out. This time her cries mingled with Logan's raw groan as he drove into her, nothing gentle or refined, pure naked desire and need fulfilled.

Nine

Logan woke with a princess in his bed. Definitely a first. An X-rated fairy tale. His own new spin on *Lady and the Tramp.* He studied her face, softened and vulnerable with sleep. And he remembered the passion that flared between them last night. Perhaps he should have treated her with more respect, more reverence, but that choice hadn't been one he could make, nor had it been one she seemed to want.

Who knew that someone so quietly elegant could inflame and return such need and desire?

When she'd first hinted at her question yesterday in the rose garden, he'd known an onslaught of emotion. Recognized it for the double-edged sword it was, full of possibilities and pitfalls. When it looked like she might turn away he'd known there was only one answer. Any other would be unthinkable.

She had chosen him. He was humbled yet wanted to beat his chest and roar his euphoric victory.

From the time of her question, he'd been consumed by thoughts of her. Not that she hadn't already taken up an undue amount of mental space. Not that he hadn't already had fantasies. But suddenly the possibilities were real and imminent. And the pitfalls enormous.

She stirred beside him, her lips full and gently curving as though her dreams were pleasant.

Last night as he'd sat alone, he'd played his guitar—it was what he did when he needed to think. He had time to consider, to wonder—the whys of what she was asking, and whether she knew what she was getting into, and whether she was as innocent and guileless as she seemed or was in fact toying with him.

He almost hoped it was the latter. That would be simpler.

He'd put down his guitar and strolled to his window. And instead of the city view he'd seen her car. She sat in it for the longest time and he watched for the longest time, and smiled as he imagined her arguing it out with herself. She'd come this far, would she take that final step?

In the end, it occurred to him that there could be other reasons for her presence there, troubles or concerns. His mind had been so firmly on its single track that it had taken too long to think of that. So he'd called her.

Gone to her.

The sweet guilt and uncertainty on her face had given him her reason for being there.

And so they'd walked. He didn't want her feeling guilty, and he didn't want her uncertain. Because what was about to happen would change things between them, complicate them.

And as much as he ached to know her, he didn't want to

lose what they already had. More than an understanding, closer to friendship. She was a glittering jewel and she sparkled for him. She was like no one he'd known before.

He looked at her now and could only hope that she woke with regrets, agreeing that it shouldn't have happened and adamant that it couldn't happen again. That they would do their best to carry on just as they had been. It might just be possible.

They could have no future, they didn't belong in each other's worlds.

Somewhere in the night she'd talked about going back to the palace. He'd pulled her toward him and convinced her that his bed was a far better place to be.

But that was then.

He made to slide from that same bed, thinking for the first time in hours with his brain, and one that wasn't completely addled with desire.

This could be awkward. Mornings after a first time always held that potential. Particularly when it was a liaison that could have no future.

A delicate hand flattened itself low on his abdomen. Her lips curled softly upward and her eyes opened, something shy and vulnerable shining in them. Hopes and dreams. And expectations. He was going to have to hurt her. They had to wind back the clock. And he had to be the one to tell her.

She'd said only that she wanted him to teach her things and he'd agreed. He'd never have been able to refuse because hell, she turned him inside out with desire. But she was a princess. It kept coming back to that. That and the fact that, for all the royal hauteur she displayed, inside was someone far more vulnerable, someone who might think she only wanted to learn the ways of desire, but someone who deserved, and he suspected needed, to be cherished. One who believed in fairy tales and happy ever afters.

Her hand slid tentatively lower.

He had to tell her. Now. His throat ran dry.

Long lashes dropped to screen her eyes as the hand slid lower still to wrap around the hard length of him. And he knew that he was a thousand kinds of bastard because he couldn't stop himself from reaching for her. She rolled toward him.

He was so doomed.

He wanted to watch her in the soft morning light. He wanted to see her naked beauty, her hair swinging, her eyes glazing over with passion, he wanted to grip the curve of hips as she rode him.

He wanted to satisfy her, to give her this one simple pleasure.

And so he said nothing. And then as she moved over and onto him knew that in the onslaught of sensation speech wasn't possible.

But he could give her tenderness, and completion, this woman of beauty and uncertainty who deserved so much better than him.

She lay pressed against him, her hair draped across his shoulder, spilling onto the pillow, and he could have sworn their hearts beat exactly in tune, gradually slowing. He had no idea what she was thinking, probably that was for the best. He hardly knew what he thought himself, other than the awareness that he'd gotten into a mess from which he needed to extricate himself. But it was the most divinely blissful mess he'd ever been in.

"I'd like—" she said quietly, then said no more.

He turned his head. She was watching him and before he knew it he'd pressed a gentle kiss to her softly parted lips, then pulled back. "What would you like?" Right now he'd give her the world.

She caught her bottom lip in her teeth. "I'd like to make you breakfast."

That wasn't what he'd been expecting. "Sure."

"But…"

"But what?"

"I haven't done it often. You might have to help me. Which I know sort of defeats the purpose. Only this one time, though. After I've done it once I'll be fine for the next time."

Just like last night.

And then as though realizing what she'd said she caught her lip again, looked away.

A woman in his bed, and not just any woman but a princess, and not just any princess, but Rebecca, and she wanted to cook for him—with his help. Maybe other magic had gone on last night than that which had occurred between the sheets.

"Sure." Breakfast, and then he'd tell her.

"I'll just shower first. Will you wait for me?" She waited for his nod and then slid from the bed. His gaze stayed glued to the pale length of her back, the sweetly rounded behind as she walked from his room. She glanced back over her shoulder and a slow sweet smile curved her lips.

He didn't wait for her. He joined her in the shower. Joined with her.

Bright morning sunlight gleamed on the kitchen's dark granite surfaces and shined in Rebecca's hair as she measured ingredients into a bowl, humming to the song playing on the radio. Logan sat at the breakfast bar watching her. She'd had a change of clothes in her car, claiming that a princess was always prepared. He'd brought the bag up for her this morning. A blue sleeveless top in some kind of silky fabric and the jeans that she really ought to wear more often. She had a figure made for jeans.

She didn't want him to do anything to help her. Except tell her how to do everything.

She'd sought…instruction last night, too. Asking him what pleased him, seeming almost uncertain about what best pleased her even, but taking delight in finding out. A quick and enthusiastic learner.

She'd wanted to make pancakes, like they'd had their first breakfast together. Logan sipped the coffee he'd made. There was something wrong with the concept and it took him a while to figure out what was sending the whispers of unease along his spine.

The domesticity, the remembrance of their first breakfast, it spoke of something more permanent than either of them had signed up for. Fear shafted through him. Fear that he could like this too much, that it filled something in him he hadn't realized was empty.

But she seemed so happy, so relaxed, that he wanted her to have this morning. Besides, she knew, just as well as he did, what they did and didn't have.

And if he was honest, he wanted it for himself, too.

Frowning in concentration, she measured ingredients.

The fact he wanted it, too, was what convinced him to move out of the kitchen. He opened his laptop on the dining table, forcing himself to read through emails and check the markets rather than watch her. Watch her hands, watch her face, watch everything about her.

She didn't understand, wouldn't because she'd had so little experience of relationships, how they worked and how they ended. How you had to not let yourself be drawn in. You had to keep a part of yourself separate and walled off. A part that watched, from a remote—safe—internal distance.

"Who taught you to cook?" She looked over her shoulder, a smudge of flour on her jaw.

"I taught myself."

She threw a puzzled glance his way. "Are your parents both still in Chicago?"

"In a manner of speaking. They're buried there."

"Oh. I'm sorry." She rested the wooden spoon in the mixing bowl and took a step toward him, her face crestfallen.

"It's okay." He held up his hand in a stop gesture. "I don't need your sympathy." And when he saw her stiffen ever so slightly at his words, he had to try to soften them. "It was a long time ago."

She turned back to the bowl, began stirring. "How long?"

"I was nineteen. My brothers were seventeen and fifteen."

"But you have three brothers."

"The twins were fifteen."

She stopped stirring. "What did you do? What happened to you all?"

"Jack and I were old enough to take care of the twins. And we had my grandparents close by." Though to be honest his grandparents had been more of a hindrance than a help—always criticizing, always negative. It was, he knew, their way of trying to help. It just hadn't been a particularly helpful way. "Anyway, my mom had done all the cooking when we were growing up and I mean all of it. She loved cooking, saw it as her role. It was her way of showing her love for us. Consequently there was a steep learning curve including lots of disasters and as many take-out meals as we could afford. But we got there."

"So, you're close to your brothers?"

"Yeah." It was something of a cliché but they'd made it through the tough times together, not without their share of drama, but those same tough times had brought them closer, made them stronger. They didn't live in each other's pockets, apart from the twins, but they were all there for each other. He watched Rebecca ladling batter into the pan, hoped she was done with the personal stuff and started thinking about ways of distracting her if she wasn't. He had to pull his own thoughts back into line. The here and now. That's where they should be. "When bubbles form and burst, you can turn them," he said.

"Do you want children?" She didn't look up.

Okay. Not done with the personal stuff. Not by a long shot.

She looked up now, biting her lip. "Sorry. I should never have asked that. It's like because we've…" She waved her hand in the air. "I've forgotten where the boundaries are." She turned back to the pan, a delicate pink blush rising up her cheeks. "And just so you know, it's not like I was thinking that because we…slept together I'm now wanting to be the mother of your children or anything." She glanced at him again. Biting her lip again but this time it looked like she was doing it to stop from laughing. "I'm making this worse, aren't I?"

He nodded because for a moment dread had welled up. But his first reaction, before the dread had swamped it, had been a flicker of something more primal, something almost the opposite of dread.

"Honestly, don't worry, and stop frowning. Once you're gone and things get back to normal and Dad gives me the space to live my own life, I'm going to find my own nice man and do with him all the things we—" She pressed elegant flour-dusted fingers over her lips. "That's so not the thing to say, either. What have you done to me?"

Apparently only things she was already planning on doing with somebody else. "It's no big deal," he said, trying to get this conversation back to a semblance of normality, trying to be okay with the thought of her with another man. "Yeah, I'd like kids someday. When I'm not so driven by the business, when I meet the right woman and the time is right." And that was enough talking about him and some imaginary future. "How about you?"

Rebecca set plates on the counter. "I used to think, no. That I didn't want to bring children up the way my brothers and I were brought up—by a succession of nannies and staff, no matter how kind and well-educated they were, and constantly in the public eye, but…"

"But?"

"Since Rafe married he's been finding ways to keep out of the limelight when it suits him, which is more and more often these days. And Lexie's pregnant. Which is great news for them but for me, too, because it means that instead of third in line to the throne, I'll be fourth. And then if they have other children and Adam marries and has children I get further and further down the line of succession."

"You don't mind?"

"Mind? No, I've been looking forward to it for years. It means that interest in me—what I'm doing and wearing and saying, and who I'm seeing—will fall off. My life will become more my own. And I sometimes wonder if then perhaps I can be a mother. A normal one. If maybe I could have children and they could have a chance at a life that approaches normal. We could cook pancakes together." She smiled, but the smile dimmed. "But I'm not even sure I'll know how to be a mother. I have so few memories of my own. And—" she looked up "—that's way more than you wanted to know. I'm sorry. I shouldn't have dumped all that on you. I don't even know where it all came from. What I should have said was, yes. Just yes, or maybe. One day. What's really weird about all of this is that usually I know the right things to say and, more importantly, I usually know when to stop talking."

She looked suddenly uncomfortable, this woman in his kitchen with a dusting of flour on her lips. "Strikes me that any kid would be lucky to have you for a mom." Even luckier would be the man who got to make those babies with her.

"Thank you." She frowned at the pancakes. "I shouldn't have talked so much about myself, though."

"Why not?"

"It's not good manners, it's not good conversation. I should have asked more about you."

"Because it's good manners?" he asked, offended.

"Yes. Tell me about—"

"Don't you dare ask me something just because it's good manners. I'd far rather talk about you. I'd far rather talk to that woman I just got a glimpse of. The one who's a person with fears and insecurities and not a perfect princess."

She smiled. She really had a beautiful smile. It lit her whole face. "If it's fears and insecurities you want I can give you those by the bucketful." She turned back to the pan and flipped a pancake.

He wanted to kiss her. Wanted to cross to her and take her in his arms, take her back to his bed. Which made him want to kick himself. They'd transitioned from what they had—something safe—to this, which he couldn't quite define, but which felt like the slipperiest of slopes.

He glanced at the screen in front of him. He'd pulled up the home page of the *San Philippe Times*. It was covered in photos of the two of them at the rose gardens. "The press are taking the bait." It wouldn't hurt to keep to the forefront the fact that this was a charade. Admittedly one with benefits.

"Oh." She didn't look up from the pan. "Great."

He scrolled through the photos on-screen. The two of them at the rose garden, sitting close, leaning slightly toward each other. The two of them walking, looking at each other—the heat clear to see. The two of them kissing and then finally… "Damn."

"What is it?"

"A photo of your car on the road outside. They got it before I shifted it."

Rebecca lifted one slender shoulder in a shrug. "It wouldn't have been difficult. It was out there for a while."

"I should have shifted it sooner. I'm sorry." The politeness and awkwardness was creeping in. He should welcome it, not regret it. Not want to take them back just half an hour to when they were in bed.

"It was hardly your fault. I drove here. I parked it there. Besides, ultimately my life will be easier with just a smidgen of tarnish on my reputation. The whole Perfect Princess thing is pretty hard to live up to. So long as I ultimately get that engagement ring. The fake one," she added quickly, as though to reassure him she wasn't still thinking futures and babies. "Everything will be fine."

He kept his focus on the screen, annoyed nonetheless. "There are some things the whole country doesn't need to know about." Their private life for one thing, because what they'd shared last night, for all that it had a purpose and limits, was private. It had been between them. Not to further either of their causes.

"The thing with publicity is that while you can influence it, ultimately you don't get to choose." She flipped another pancake.

"I know."

"They'd be thinking it anyway," she said carefully. "And it is what we wanted, isn't it? We have this intense relationship, we get engaged, we break up."

"True. But it should have been better planned, better controlled. And I'm not sure you realize that once the tarnish is there it's hard to get rid of."

Rebecca all but rolled her eyes. "You're seriously trying to explain to me about reputations?"

"Preaching to the choir?"

"The millionth sermon on the subject."

"I just feel bad for your lack of privacy. That you can't do anything without people knowing about it."

She shrugged. "When you don't have a choice you do it. Probably you would have said when you were eighteen that you weren't able to raise three brothers but you did. This is just how my life is. Besides, people need to think things are progressing fast and well between us so that our engagement is believable and so that they're on my side when it ends."

"So, you're just using me?"

She smiled. A man could grow to count on those smiles. "Yes. I'm using you."

"If that's being used," he said, "I'm all for it." He returned his attention to the computer screen. He had to, otherwise he'd be out of his chair and letting her use him all over again.

"You were very good, you know. I enjoyed it. A lot."

"Rebecca."

She looked at him.

"You're not analyzing, remember." All the same he

knew that together they had been much better than good.
It was a definite chemistry thing.

She smiled. So sweet. So unbelievably sweet. "Seems
like, if somebody gives you a gift, you should say thank
you. So I'd just wanted to say—"

"Don't. Don't you dare." Because if there were thanks
to be given it wasn't her who should be giving them.

He read a couple of the captions and some of the accom-
panying text. "They're definitely going to be on your side
if what I'm reading is anything to go by. They're happy
that their 'lonely' princess has found love." He almost
stumbled over that last word. That was exactly what they
wanted people to think, but to see it in black and white
and applied to him and Rebecca, it seemed wrong. The fact
that this was indeed playing out exactly as they'd wanted
seemed wrong.

"I don't know why they're always insisting I'm lonely."

"That's the bit that irks you?"

"Being on your own does not make you lonely." Her
hands fisted on her hips. An irate, beautiful chef/princess
in his kitchen. Almost all too much to process. His brothers
would laugh their heads off.

Speaking of which, he'd undoubtedly have to let them
know something was up. They hated reading stuff about
him in the papers before he'd told them. Although they
probably wouldn't credit this particular story for a while,
writing it off instead as the media getting things utterly
wrong again as they so often had in the past. In fact, the
whole affair could be over before any of them picked up
on it.

His phone rang. He considered ignoring it but so few
people had his personal number he picked it up instead.
Besides, he needed to remember this was just a charade.
They didn't need cozy, intimate mornings in his kitchen.

If they weren't making love, or being seen in public, he told himself, then there was no good reason for her to be here. And then he felt like a prize jerk for even having that thought.

"Logan," he snapped into the phone.

"What's eating you?" a deep voice retorted.

"Jack?" Logan picked up his coffee and strolled to the window, preparing himself for the inevitable. Sunlight glistened on the slow moving river. "That was quick. I thought you guys would ignore the papers for a while."

"What was quick? What's in the papers? I haven't seen them in days."

Which wasn't unusual for Jack. He lived in a cabin in the foothills of the Sierra Nevadas, thriving on shutting himself off from the world. He could have an in-depth conversation with Rebecca about how being alone did *not* mean you were lonely. But at least for now Logan had a reprieve. "Nothing. But if it's not the papers why are you ringing?"

"Because I want you to let me in. I'm downstairs."

It took a moment for that to sink in.

Logan watched Rebecca watching him as he turned from punching the access code to allow Jack entry. "We've got company."

She tensed and took a step back, though how far she thought she could get in the confines of his kitchen was a mystery. "The papers are one thing." She shook her head as she spoke, her gray eyes wide. "Who?"

"My brother."

The tension lifted from her face, to be replaced by curiosity. Logan headed for the marbled foyer as the elevator door slid open. He could hardly block his brother. Wouldn't actually want to. But for all that, his timing sucked.

"What are you doing here?" he asked as the doors opened.

Jack strolled past him. "Good to see you, too." He walked into the apartment. "I had a meeting in London. I thought I'd call in seeing as I was in the neighborhood, so to speak." He dropped a duffel bag to the floor and walked farther into the apartment. "You don't mind if I crash here for a while." He tossed a jacket onto the couch. "And did you know there's a photographer outside taking pictures of your place?" He turned for the kitchen and stopped when he saw Rebecca. "And I'm guessing you know there's a woman in your kitchen."

Rebecca gave a tentative smile and lifted the spatula in a greeting.

"Yeah. I had noticed," Logan said, quelling his own smile as he watched Rebecca. A hint of color climbed her face. Sweet. It was intriguing the way she managed to keep surprising him. So few women did. "Rebecca, this is my brother Jack. And Jack, this is—" He didn't know if there was a way he was supposed to introduce royalty, but he'd never been one to follow protocol and he wasn't going to start now. "Rebecca."

Jack studied her. "You look familiar. Did you ever live in Chicago?"

"No."

Jack shrugged then looked at Logan, speculation and a question in his gaze. "I should go, right?"

"No," they said in unison. She sounded almost as relieved as he was to have Jack here. Which was weird given than she'd instigated the whole let-me-make-breakfast routine.

"In fact," Rebecca said, "I should go."

This time it was Jack's turn to protest, but it was Logan she watched so he added his denial to his brother's.

"Rebecca's a fine cook." She raised her eyebrows and shot a worried glance at the fry pan then whirled with a gasp.

"Smells…interesting," Jack said.

And there was, Logan admitted, a definite hint of charcoal in the air. "Second batch always turns out better than the first," he said as he stepped into the kitchen, effectively blocking her exit when it looked like she might bolt. He held her shoulders. "Ignore Jack." He tipped the burned pancake into the trash, set the pan back on the stove and gestured to the bowl of batter. "Second time's a charm."

"I'll just take a shower," Jack called, then turned and walked away.

"I really should go." Rebecca looked past Logan.

"No."

She stiffened. "Are you telling me what I can and can't do?"

"The royal outrage is cute, Princess, but I'm telling you you're not leaving now. If that's what you're asking."

"But—"

He shifted her hair to expose her neck then kissed her, and though he hadn't yet gotten to her lips he'd effectively cut off her words. It was the only way he could think of to silence her protests. But just for good measure he found her lips, too. Let himself savor the gentlest of kisses. And effectively derailed his own train of thought, as well. One moment he was thinking only of soothing the panic that looked about to bloom into royal hauteur, and the next moment the taste of her, her soft warm mouth beneath his, had him remembering all the things they'd done together last night. All the things they could do again and the things they had yet to do. He'd need—not a lifetime, never that— but it could certainly take all of the remaining weeks they had left.

Ten

Rebecca sat at the table with two big and largely silent men, both intent on eating. If there was anything wrong with her pancakes, they were doing a good job of hiding it. That much about this morning gave her a sense of satisfaction. She rarely cooked for herself. Living in the palace it just wasn't necessary. There was something elementally satisfying about watching Logan and his brother eat.

But she couldn't dwell on the satisfaction because this was all wrong. She should have left last night. She'd wanted Logan to share the benefit of his experience with her—which he'd been more than generous in doing. So much so that she hadn't been able to leave. She'd been enthralled. But there had been no talk of mornings after. She had what she thought she'd wanted. She should be content with that and go. Except he'd stopped her when she'd tried. Good manners only? She didn't know and could hardly ask.

"So, Jack. Logan never mentioned he had a brother coming to San Philippe."

Jack set down his fork. "Logan always plays his cards close to his chest. But in this case it's because he didn't know. But more importantly he didn't mention to me or either of our other brothers that he was seeing a beautiful woman. Which is a perfect example of what I mean about the cards and their closeness to his chest. Very secretive, my brother. Hates people knowing what he's doing."

"Feel free to address your questions and observations directly to me," Logan muttered.

"Thanks. How long have you two been an item?" Jack asked.

"Oh, we're not really—"

"A few weeks," Logan said. "I was going to let you know."

Jack shrugged. "I'm not surprised you haven't. You two clearly had other more important things to do."

Rebecca turned her attention to cutting a slice off her pancake. People—other than Logan—didn't usually make such blatant innuendos around her.

"Jack." Logan's voice was a low warning. Another hint of that unexpected chivalry, the one that had surfaced when he'd been concerned for her reputation.

Jack looked up, genuinely surprised. "What? There's a woman in your kitchen cooking you breakfast, both of you look like you had a damn fine night. You have that glow about you. The one I haven't had in far too long. What else am I supposed to think? Since when did you get so prissy anyway?" Jack reached for his coffee.

"Since I started dating a damn princess is when."

Jack coughed, trying and failing to contain the coffee he'd just sipped. He reached for a napkin to mop up the table.

"I don't expect people to change for me," Rebecca insisted.

Jack studied his brother. "A princess. I knew you were moving in high circles but how did that happen?"

Rebecca looked to Logan for the explanation. She didn't know which version of their story he wanted to give his brother. The spin or the truth?

Whichever, Logan wasn't looking thrilled with his brother. "We met here a few times and then I ran into Rebecca in New Zealand."

"You'd been visiting the Coromandel properties?"

Oh, great. He'd really had business in New Zealand. She'd all but called him a liar over that.

"Yes." Logan winked at her, enjoying her discomfort. "And it turns out we have a few things in common—" he shrugged "—and one thing led to another and so here we are."

So, a version somewhere between the spin and the truth.

"Here you are," Jack said slowly. "Can't hurt with your plans to expand into Europe."

"No."

Jack looked at Rebecca. "No matter what success he achieved at home he always wanted Europe. Always wanted to prove a point to the old man, our grandfather," he explained, looking at Rebecca. "Nothing any of us ever did was good enough for him. And being German, Europe was the acme of achievement. I think maybe dating a princess would impress even him."

"Good to know I could be of use," Rebecca said mildly.

"It's a bit late, he's dead now," Jack added, "but the conditioning lives on."

"And I really do have to get going." Rebecca stood. Logan and Jack both stood, too.

"Nice meeting you, Rebecca." Jack smiled and shook

his head. "My brother and a princess. Never would have seen that one coming. Does this mean I could have a nephew who's king of San Philippe one day?"

"No," Logan said. "Because San Philippe is a principality not a kingdom."

"There's a difference?" Jack asked.

Logan shook his head in mock despair. "Kingdoms have kings, principalities have princes. Look it up."

"And," Rebecca continued, "because your brother is just using me for my connections and I'm using him for his body. There's nothing permanent." Her version of the truth.

"I'm not sure that you're getting the better half of that deal." Jack laughed and puffed out a chest as broad as Logan's, folding his arms so that his biceps bulged against the sleeves of his gray T-shirt. "Now if it's a fine body and a fine mind you're after…" He winked.

Rebecca laughed though Logan didn't look to find his brother as amusing as she did. She linked her arm through his, an arm that had held her so tenderly last night. "I'm pretty satisfied with my side of the deal so far."

"I'll walk you to your car. Say goodbye, Jack."

She extricated her arm. "Just give me a minute. I need to freshen up a little and get my bag."

In Logan's bedroom she barely spared a glance for that big, big bed where she'd spent the best night of her life. Instead she gathered up her things and dropped them into her bag. In the bathroom she tidied herself up, put on a little makeup. Outside, she could hear low voices. They weren't exactly arguing but there was definitely a discussion of sorts going on. As she left the room she caught Jack's voice. "What are you trying to prove to the old man? He's dead anyway."

"It's not that."

"Come on. This need of yours to always be the best. Doesn't get much better than royalty."

"Keep out of it, Jack." Logan's voice was low and serious. "She's not royalty. She's a woman."

Rebecca was oddly touched by the distinction.

"I can see that—"

Rebecca didn't know what Logan said or did but Jack stopped speaking for a moment. "Oh. So have you given her the I-can't-let-a-relationship-interfere-with-business speech?"

"No. This is different," Logan said abruptly, clearly not enjoying the conversation.

"Okay. Wow. Sorry. She must really mean a lot to you."

"No." His denial was quick and emphatic.

"You're not fooling me. Your guitar's out. You never play for other people."

"I didn't play for her. She doesn't mean anything to me."

Rebecca walked around the corner. She would have stopped and waited if she'd known those were the words she was going to walk around to.

Both men turned to look at her. Only one of them, Logan, cursed. "I'm sorry. I didn't mean—"

What? He didn't mean that? He didn't mean to say it? Or he just didn't mean for her to hear it? She'd never know because he didn't finish the sentence. Her lover of last night, the one whose words alone had lit fires within her, seemed lost for words.

But she was a princess so it was okay. Because she could smile through anything, look dignified through anything.

"Jack, it's been a pleasure meeting you. Logan, I can see myself to the car. Please stay with your brother."

She turned to go. Regal, refined, letting no emotions show. She could do it. Though she'd never had to fight quite so hard for calm before, to walk serenely when she wanted to run, to smile over the gasp of pain that had threatened to escape.

Logan caught up to her. Stepped into the elevator with her before she could shut the doors.

"Rebecca..." Her name on his lips resonated with remorse.

"It's okay, Logan. I'm not supposed to mean anything to you. Though you could have at least waited until I left the apartment. It kind of ruined what had been a very nice night." There was the understatement of the year. Two of them. *Kind of* ruined and *nice*.

He faced her, turned her to face him. "It scared me when Jack said you must mean something to me because I don't want you to mean anything to me. I don't want what we have to mean anything. Because it's going to end. But whether I want it to or not, it does mean something. It means a lot. You have to know that. You don't spend a night like last night with someone—and I'm talking about all of it, the walking by the river, the meal and the making love—without it meaning something. And this morning."

She wanted so desperately to believe him. She just didn't know if she could. "I'll have to take your word for it. You'll have noticed that my experience isn't quite on the same plane as yours."

"Then do take my word for it."

"Thank you. I will. You're very kind."

"Hell, Rebecca, stop that."

"I'm trying to be gracious."

"I know. That's what I want you to stop."

"You'd rather I ranted and raved."

"Yes."

She studied him a moment, silencing the part of her that

could too easily rant and rave. She was better than that. "Well, you don't get what you want. Not this time."

"And you've never said something you wanted to be true even though you knew it wasn't. Something like, 'That didn't hurt Logan, those words didn't cut. I'm not upset.'"

"Can we stop this?"

"No. Not yet. Not until you believe I didn't mean what I said to Jack."

The elevator stopped and the doors opened to the parking garage and Rebecca stepped out. "It doesn't matter."

Logan walked with her. "It matters."

"In that case I do believe you. And I'm not just saying that to placate you or saying something I want to be true even though I know it's not. Because last night meant something to me. And although it can't possibly have meant as much to you, it had to mean something. Didn't it?"

They stopped at her car. Logan stood in front of her door, blocking her escape.

"It did." He said the words so simply. His gaze open and intense, as though he was willing her to look into his eyes and believe him. He shouldn't be allowed to have such beautiful eyes. "It. *You*. Mean a lot more than just something."

A terrible sadness welled within her, threatened to break loose.

She leaned forward and kissed him, a touch of her lips to his just because she could. And because she couldn't not. And then she stepped back. "See you at the polo." They could go on from here. Go on with their deal. She would keep seeing him in public. She might even kiss him in public. But that—what she'd just done—was their last private kiss. She could almost wish it had been longer so that she'd have more than the memory of a fleeting taste of coffee and maple syrup, of firm lips, of fledgling warmth.

"You're okay? You'll be there?"

"You flatter yourself, Logan, if you think just one night with you could be so affecting that it would change everything."

So who was lying now? The voice of honesty taunted her.

He reached for her, gripped her shoulders and lowered his head to hers, gave her more of a memory, beguiled and enchanted her with his kiss as he seemed so effortlessly able to do. She, on the other hand, had to make an effort. An effort not to melt into him, not to wrap her arms around him and hold him close.

He pulled back, his hands had slipped up to frame her face and he held her head still while he studied her, held her gaze. "You mean more to me than is good for me."

Finally he released her and stepped aside to open her door.

She got in, put her key in the ignition and forced herself to think clearly and without emotion or sentiment. They'd get engaged—and she would not let it mean anything—and then they would break up. That time couldn't come soon enough. Because if this morning's debacle had taught her anything, breaking up with him was not going to be easy. At least not for her.

He closed her door and she lowered the window and looked up at him. It had to be said. "I wanted to say thank you."

"Thank you?" He practically growled the words. "Don't you dare."

"Good manners dictate it." She glanced at his fingers tightening on her door frame. "I made a request of you. And you more than satisfied that request."

"You think that's the end of it?"

"It has to be."

He stepped back and folded his arms across his chest. And for the first time since she'd heard him talking to his brother, a flicker of the amusement she was so used to flashed in his eyes as he shook his head. "See you at the polo then. But just so you know, that's not the end of it. Not by a long shot."

Eleven

Rebecca stood at the front of the royal enclosure. Usually she loved watching polo, the drama of the thundering hoofbeats. And she'd seen Logan play before. He was a natural horseman with an uncanny ability to read the game, to be in the right place at the right time. He'd told her how he'd learned to ride working vacations on a relative's ranch but that he'd come to the game itself comparatively late.

Today she had to split herself in two to watch the match. She had to appear to be fascinated because she needed to convince the throng of people in the marquee that Logan captivated her. In particular she wanted to convince her father, holding court in the enclosure, and the bachelors here from his list who were trickling into the country.

The impromptu ball was fast approaching. She needed her relationship with Logan to look solid, she needed to look infatuated. But at the same time she needed to not be infatuated. Infatuation being a state that might well be easy to slip into. So she watched with determined detachment. And though she tried to concentrate on her brothers, who were both on the team, it was Logan who drew her eye. *I will not admire his skill. I will not admire his seat, in either the equestrian or the bodily sense of the word.* Detachment. She practically had to repeat the word like some kind of mantra.

He had phoned her last night, his voice warm and gentle over the line. He'd called, not to ask anything of her, not to rehash the mess the morning had turned into. But just, he'd said, to hear her voice, to know that she was okay.

She had wanted to go to him. To ask him to come to her. She had wanted the balm of being in his arms. But she managed to keep those needy words at bay, and to just bask in the warm cocoon that had surrounded her. That, she'd decided was his skill, the ability he had, even over the phone, to establish a connection that felt exclusive as though he thought only of her.

The opposing team scored a goal, leveling the score.

Various people—too many of them male and eligible—tried to claim her attention. But that wasn't what she wanted, either. So she positioned herself close to Lexie, who, like the boys in the team Rafe coached, cheered raucously, focusing intently on every play of the game.

Standing on the other side of Lexie, watching with no enthusiasm but looking stunning, was Adam's latest date, a young Hollywood actress.

Logan sped around an opposing player, swung his mallet and scored a goal, turned and cantered past her. She couldn't help but watch him, irritated with herself that his wink seemed just for her, threatened to warm her. She could feel what was happening and she wouldn't let it.

She would not fall for him. Something that one-sided would be sheer stupidity.

Lexie nudged her arm. "I didn't think he was going to get that last goal, he spends so much time looking over at you. But I guess that gives him all the more incentive to try to impress."

"He doesn't need to impress me."

"Because you're already impressed?"

"No. Because he's not the sort to try to impress, and I'm not the sort to be impressed by sporting prowess."

"What about by a fine body?" Lexie nudged again, drawing out a smile.

"Maybe a little." She watched that fine body as he rose up in his stirrups, lean-hipped, in nicely fitting whites. She sighed and dragged her gaze away.

Lexie's eyes danced in knowing amusement. "Great seat."

"How's the pregnancy going?" Rebecca asked pointedly, eager to change the subject.

Lexie leaped on the change. "I'm feeling terrific." She pressed her hand to her abdomen. "We're going to announce it soon." Lexie turned when one of the boys from Rafe's team approached her.

Rafe's whirlwind courtship and marriage to Lexie had surprised everyone, including Rafe. But the fact that the two of them were deliriously happy was plain to see. And Rebecca couldn't be more pleased for them. But she also couldn't help wondering whether she'd ever find that kind of soul-deep love, that kind of happiness. She looked over at Logan—to whom she meant nothing—and looked away again. Her heart sank further as she saw Eduardo walking purposefully toward her.

"Things going well with you and Buchanan?"

"Good game, don't you think?" She gestured at the

field. Eduardo was the last person with whom she wanted to discuss her relationship with Logan.

"I've seen better. There's another board meeting next week, the main purpose of which is to discuss the sale of the subsidiary."

Why was he telling her? "I didn't realize you had an interest in leBlanc."

Eduardo affected boredom. "The new stepfather. Wants to do a little father-son bonding. Wants my opinion on Buchanan's character. That sort of thing."

"Oh, look. Another goal." Rebecca clapped.

Eduardo glanced at the game. "You know he's using you to further his business interests? I thought you should know."

Eduardo ought to know. He'd wanted to use her, too, to further his political aspirations. "Thank you for thinking of me. That's really very sweet of you."

Eduardo's mouth tightened. "He's not right for you."

Rebecca hid her surprise at Eduardo's intrusion into her privacy. He was usually more subtle. Warning prickled along her skin.

"He's never going to fit into the kind of life we lead. He doesn't understand it. Doesn't approve of it. And he doesn't play by the rules."

It took effort to keep her voice neutral, to not leap to Logan's defense. "Thank you for your opinion. You are, as always, right." What he failed to understand was that was part of Logan's appeal, and Rebecca couldn't like any "we" that bracketed her with Eduardo. "Now, if you'll let me watch the match."

Eduardo's eyes went cold. "I apologize for my interruption. I was only trying to help. We've been friends for a long time. And I'll still be here after he's gone."

"We have been friends for a long time. So please don't spoil it."

"I'd do anything not to spoil it. But I need to talk to you. And for your boyfriend's sake it should be before the board meeting." There was something about the way Eduardo was speaking that chilled her, made her think that she hardly knew this man she'd known for most of her life. A couple of members of one of the visiting polo teams approached. Eduardo leaned closer and spoke quietly. "I need to talk to you in private. Soon."

"Make an appointment with my secretary."

Eduardo, displeasure curling his lip, nodded then turned and strode away.

Five minutes later the final chukker was over and still she watched Logan, surrounded by well-wishers, people wanting to congratulate him on the winning goal, wanting to revel in the reflected glory, to share in the team's jubilation. She kept her distance and chatted with other spectators. She caught his gaze a couple of times when he looked her way, both times as he'd looked at her his smile had faded. He left with his teammates to shower and change. She would have gone then, too, if it hadn't been expected that she'd wait. She'd be being watched, analyzed. They were supposed to be a couple. And if she was a true girlfriend, one who meant something—she couldn't help the mental aside—she would stay. An early departure would draw attention. The wrong sort.

She was still speaking with the polo players when she felt a familiar tingle along her spine and turned to see Logan approaching, his gaze intent on her. And then he was at her side, smiling as he apologized to the players and various other people wanting to speak with both of them as he led her away.

She let out a sigh and wasn't sure whether it was relief at escaping the artifice or pleasure at being with him.

The worrying thought was it might be the latter. She liked being with him too much. It was something beyond logic, beyond control. It just was.

"Watch the Argentinean player. Number eight. He's a player in all senses of the word," Logan said.

"But charming to speak with and he has quite the sense of humor. Slightly wicked but very funny nonetheless." She could look after herself.

Logan sighed.

They walked past the hospitality marquees brimming with guests sipping champagne and around to the players' side of the fields. Horse trucks were parked in long rows; beside them grooms brushed down tethered polo ponies and unwound and deftly rolled up the protective bandages from their legs.

She'd always liked the smell of horses, warm and earthy. Now it combined with the scent of the freshly showered man at her side, one of soap and spice.

They walked side by side, not talking. Arms occasionally brushing. He caught her hand in his.

"I'm glad you came," he said finally.

"I said I would."

"I thought I'd ruined it yesterday." Regret tinged his voice.

"You did. But I needed the warning." She was trying to show him that she had things in perspective, even if she wasn't sure she did, and she was trying to assure him that she wasn't upset. They could continue with their charade like two rational adults.

"Dammit, Rebecca."

She glanced at him and raised her eyebrows. It wasn't like him to curse in her presence. But still it gave her a small sense of satisfaction that he'd lost some of his composure. "Dammit? Really?"

"And don't get all prissy on me."

"I'm not getting *prissy,* I just thought we'd lifted our game when we started dating a princess." She knew her use of the royal *we* would irk him. But hadn't he said as much to his brother? And hadn't she insisted she didn't expect people to change for her?

"You're driving me nuts."

"It's mutual." They strolled up a gentle rise and stopped under the shade of an oak tree, turning back to watch the activity around the horse trucks a short distance away. "We can call an early end to this whole thing if that would suit you better?" She needed to put that option out there for him.

And suddenly his arm was around her shoulders and he swung her in close and kissed her. Angry and hungry and wanting. And—dammit—she needed his kiss so badly. Needed it because it pushed through all the barriers between them. It said he did feel something for her, even exasperation was better than nothing. She leaned into him, let his mouth claim hers, let his tongue tease hers, and did her share of claiming and teasing in return. Her eyes closed so that apart from the sounds around them, her only sensations were physical—the press of him against her, his arms around her and his lips on hers. The taste and flavor of him. His warmth, his strength.

She missed what they'd lost. Craved this feeling of being in his arms, of being close, the certainty that what was between them was important, was in fact the only thing that mattered. But as soon as the kiss ended the surety evaporated.

Just yesterday she'd made a resolution to not kiss him

in private anymore. She looked about. There were people not too far away, so this kiss had definitely been allowed.

He stepped back, just a little, breathing hard. "No. It wouldn't suit me better."

Still partially dazed from their kiss she had to think back to what her question was, what wouldn't suit him. Oh. "I suppose you still need board approval. But maybe after the board meeting…"

He closed his eyes for a second, and when he opened them again he was utterly serious. "No. It still won't suit me after the meeting. We have an agreement. Our relationship lasts until after the ball." His eyes narrowed, his gaze intent on her. "What do you know about the board meeting?"

Rebecca considered telling Logan about Eduardo, but what had he really said? Only that Logan was using her and that Eduardo would be around after Logan had gone. Both facts that were out in the open. She lifted a shoulder.

"Just that it's the meeting you talked about. The one that meant you needed to be seen with my father." And look where that had got them.

"I saw you talking to Eduardo."

"Yes." She lifted her chin. "Not just the other polo players. But as far as I can recall our agreement didn't stipulate who we could and couldn't talk to."

He leaned closer, put his lips near her ear and murmured, "Prissy."

And Rebecca laughed. "Maybe just a little. But I'm allowed. It's in my job description." In so many ways Logan was good for her. She took herself too seriously sometimes. He made sure she didn't. He seemed able to ease a tension she didn't know she carried, making her laugh. And then there were the other ways in which he was good—very good—for her.

He was still close. Close enough that she could practically count the dark spiky lashes framing his eyes. He held her hands in his, touched his forehead to hers. If only this moment, the one simple connection that wasn't about anything other than just being here with him, could last forever.

Where was the distance she'd promised herself? The cool reserve?

"There's something disturbingly appealing about you when you do the royal thing, all clipped and precise with that haughty tilt to your chin. It's such an act. I can't believe more people don't see right through it."

Neither could she. But most people had no idea. It seemed only Logan saw through it. Which meant Logan was the one who saw her insecurities. But with him at least she knew they were safe.

"There you are." A booming voice interrupted. "I see you've finally taken your foot out of your mouth long enough to do something useful with it. Your mouth, that is. Not your foot."

"Yes. And you're not helping." Logan glanced at his brother. "Go away."

"Can't yet. I just met a delightful—"

"Then we will." He looked at Rebecca. "Are you ready to leave?"

She nodded, all the while knowing that she was far too ready to do whatever this man wanted of her.

Photographers snapped shots of them as they headed for his car, walking purposefully, Logan holding her hand. She couldn't imagine it would make interesting viewing for anybody.

"Where are we going?" she asked as they pulled away.

"Somewhere we can get some privacy," he said through clenched teeth. "There's something I want to do with you."

That they weren't followed, Rebecca put down to the increasing speculation about Lexie's possible pregnancy. Press hopes were for a shot of a baby bump or even a public announcement. Though there was some gossip about a potential engagement between Logan and her, theirs was perceived as the less likely and less imminent news.

But privacy with Logan? Something he wanted to do with her?

She thought back to the last time they'd had any real privacy. She looked at the line of his jaw, the small vee of tanned chest revealed by the undone top buttons of his shirt, his competent hands on the wheel, hands that had touched her so intimately, so lovingly, so…magically, and knew that he could too easily undermine her resolve to maintain a degree of physical and emotional distance.

"I don't think your apartment's a good idea."

He raised an eyebrow and a grin quirked his lips. "That's not what I had in mind."

She wanted to kick herself. That simple assumption had revealed too much about the paths her thoughts took. She might not think his apartment was a good idea, but that didn't mean it wasn't where the less sensible part of her wanted to go. "So, where?" she asked casually.

"You'll see."

"You really do like to play your cards close to your chest."

He stopped for a traffic light and brushed a knuckle along her jaw. "And you really don't like not being the one in control. Just wait. I think you'll like it."

Twelve

Half an hour later Rebecca stood smiling on the small dock as she looked at the pretty white-and-red rowboat Logan had hired for them. She glanced down at her dress and shoes, a well-coordinated ensemble in cream and beige, the shoes with the cutest heels, perfect for the polo, not so perfect for a rowboat.

"You'll be fine," Logan said, breaking into her thoughts as he came to stand beside her. "All you have to do is sit." He passed her one of the matching straw hats and then handed her into the wooden boat, and once she was seated, climbed in and sat facing her on the front seat. He nodded at the man renting them the boat, who then disappeared into the small brightly painted shed on the dock and returned a few seconds later carrying…a guitar? He handed the instrument in its soft case to Logan, who set it behind him in the boat. Logan was going to play for her. Her heart soared foolishly. The boat owner gave them a firm push off from the dock.

Logan began rowing. Here, the river, overhung with willows, moved slowly. He rowed with long, smooth strokes, taking them upstream. Sunlight sparkled on the water. The only sound was the quiet rhythmic knock of the oars in the rowlocks.

"This seemed like the best way of getting you away from the people who want to talk to us," he said as he rowed, "but we're in public, it'll still count toward the occasions we've been seen together."

In the distance visitors strolled through the rose gardens. "And very romantic-looking, too," she said, trying to sound as though she was thinking purely analytically, while not sounding cynical. "It'll definitely look good."

"Exactly."

For the sake of the balance of the boat she sat directly opposite him, her feet in their impractical heels firmly together but placed between his widely spaced feet.

She leaned over the side and trailed her fingers in the cool water, mainly to avoid looking directly at Logan. Though she couldn't help the occasional glance. For all that this ought to be relaxing, he didn't look relaxed. Didn't look to be enjoying himself any more than she was. "Can I row?" she asked.

His gaze narrowed doubtfully.

"Princesses aren't helpless, you know."

"I never thought they were. Actually, I've never given any thought to it, but I've never assumed anything of the sort about you. Quite the opposite, in fact."

"Oh. Thank you."

"Swing around to sit beside me, then I'll shift to your seat."

They completed the maneuver. Logan took the guitar

with him and Rebecca began rowing, glad to have something to do, something other than Logan to focus on. Her unpracticed efforts were clumsy at first, but Logan placed his hands beside hers on the oars, helped her get a feel for the rhythm of rowing and the placement of the oars.

He unzipped the guitar.

"You don't have to." It was enough that he'd thought to bring the guitar. A gesture she appreciated.

"I know I don't have to. I want to. You are the only person on the list of people I would play for. It's private. But this is so you know that you mean something. That what you heard me say to Jack couldn't have been further from the truth." The intensity in his gaze and the sentiment behind his words almost made her want to weep, so desperately did she want to mean something to this man.

Looking away, he settled the instrument on his thigh and began playing, his fingers moving assuredly over strings and frets. He glanced up. "Just don't expect me to sing." His smile flashed.

Rebecca rowed slowly, overhanging willows occasionally brushing the boat, and listened. His soft strumming was the perfect accompaniment to their afternoon.

Too soon he stopped and slid the guitar back into its case. "It wouldn't be right to let you do all the rowing."

"I was enjoying it. Your playing. And the rowing."

"But still. Besides, there's something we need to talk about." His voice was suddenly serious.

Rebecca concentrated on keeping the oars even, dipping them into the water simultaneously, pulling back evenly. "Is everything all right?"

"I've never done this before."

"Sat in a boat while a woman rowed?"

"Not that." Logan slid a hand into the pocket of his

trousers, pulled out a small jeweler's box and leaned toward her. "I think we should get engaged."

Her left oar skittered across the surface of the water, the boat swerved, she overcorrected and the boat spun the other way. Finally she got it back under control. She rowed with long strokes, trying to find a rhythm that suddenly eluded her. "I guess." Somehow, after the guitar playing, the offer of engagement felt like a letdown.

He still held the small velvet box in his hand. "I didn't know if I should have had you with me to choose the ring. I wasn't sure what you like. But this one appealed. I could imagine you wearing it."

Long even strokes. That was all she had to do. This wasn't a proposal. Logan wasn't asking her to marry her. Even if he had imagined her wearing the ring he'd chosen. This was just a temporary symbol of their temporary arrangement. "It doesn't really matter." She spoke the words as much to convince herself as him.

"It does matter. I want you to like it. You're the one who has to wear it."

"Makes sense," she said casually. "But it's only for a couple of weeks. Then you'll get it back." Something tightened in her throat.

"I don't want it back," he said, the words clipped, almost angry. "What am I going to do with an engagement ring?"

She glanced back over her shoulder to make sure her direction was true. And to avoid meeting Logan's gaze. "Give it to someone else? Sell it?" It wasn't easy to stop herself from looking at either Logan or the ring but she managed. She looked at her hands on the oars, the water, the riverbank. She hadn't cried in years. She wasn't going to now. She didn't even know why the sudden urge was there, tightening her jaw. It was as though this expected *proposal* had spoiled a near perfect afternoon. And yet this was precisely what they had agreed upon. But the voice of the girl she'd once been—idealistic and full of dreams—wanted to refuse, because suddenly this wasn't enough. She wanted more.

Just this morning over breakfast her father had been so relaxed, the lines that creased his brow almost permanently had eased. He'd expressed his satisfaction with her relationship with Logan.

She couldn't throw it all away now.

And besides, Logan needed her for his negotiations. To help his dreams come true. Which was precisely why he was sitting opposite her holding a small box out for her. "Are you even going to look at it?"

"Of course. If you'd like." She pulled the oars toward her, sliding them through the rowlocks so she could rest them on the edge of the boat.

When she'd run out of excuses to not look at him she lifted her gaze to his glare. This was not how engagements were supposed to happen. Even fake ones, surely.

"Of course, we'll need to talk to my father. Royal protocol and all that."

"I've spoken to him. Asked his permission. It seemed like the thing to do."

"When?"

"Yesterday afternoon."

"What did he say?" Though she knew what her father must have said, given his contentment this morning.

"I'm here, aren't I? Although he didn't say much at all. First I got one of the longest silences I've ever had to endure."

Rebecca smiled. She could just imagine it. "He's good at that."

"Very. And then he asked if I thought I could make you happy."

"Oh." She suddenly knew the answer to that, too. She looked at the peeling paint on the bottom of the boat. Logan did make her happy. Being with him was unlike being with anyone else.

"For a while there I didn't know if I could go through with it. The thought of lying to your father wasn't a good feeling. But the funny thing is that when I finally said yes, it wasn't a lie. Sometimes I think I do make you happy, when I'm not making you sad by saying stupid things to my brother. You do something…similar for me. So that bit wasn't a lie. When I told him you're the most amazing woman I've ever met, that wasn't a lie, either. It was just the wanting-to-marry-you bit that wasn't exactly the truth. But after a couple of reasonably dire threats about what will happen if I fail to make you happy, he gave me his permission. So, given what I've had to go through already, you could put an end to the torture and at least look at the ring rather than the floor of the boat. As fascinating as it is."

She looked up and met his gaze. There was something both teasing yet utterly serious in the depths of his eyes. She reached for the box, and eased open the lid. An exquisite sapphire surrounded by diamonds sparkled and glinted, full of promise and beauty. Her heart seemed to rise up in her chest, blocking her throat even further. "It's beautiful," she said.

"Do you really like it?" His voice had gentled, and contained an unfamiliar uncertainty. "I thought of you when I saw it."

Rebecca nodded.

"Can I put it on you?"

She nodded again, still looking at the ring and the

wooden floor of the boat beyond it and out of focus. She didn't know when, if ever, she'd been quite so lost for words, quite so certain that if she said something it would be utterly inadequate, or worse, utterly unintelligible.

Logan eased the box from her fingers, lifted the ring out and slid it onto her left hand. Rebecca stretched her fingers out. The ring caught the sunlight and sparkled, full of false promise.

"I can change it if you don't like it. We could choose something different together."

"No. It's beautiful."

The boat bobbed on the water. Rebecca didn't trust herself to say anything more. Because she knew, in her heart of hearts, that she had somehow fallen in love with the man opposite her. The man whose ring she was wearing. The realization appalled her.

"Shall I row?"

That might be a good idea. She nodded and they swapped seats. Logan turned the boat downstream.

"If we announce it at the official dinner tomorrow night it ought to help your chances at the board meeting."

"That's not why I did this now." He dug the oars into the water.

"Then why?"

"I had other reasons. Not all of them quite so selfish."

"I wasn't accusing you of being selfish. I was just trying to look at the positives."

"Because otherwise it would be a negative?" He pulled hard on the oars.

"No. That's not what I said, either."

Logan heaved a sigh. "Next time I propose to a woman I'm going to do a much better job of it."

"I hope so." She managed a smile, though the thought of Logan proposing properly to a woman he loved and wanted to spend his life with did not please her. If anything quite the opposite. She bit her lip.

Logan stopped rowing and pulled in the oars, letting the boat drift with the current. His legs bracketed hers and he leaned forward, slid his hands along her jaw. His thumbs stroked over her cheekbones, and for long seconds she just looked into his beautiful brown eyes, and then he pulled her closer to kiss her. And his kiss did what it always did—broke through the maze of barriers, to something simple and lovely.

There was a kernel deep within her that ached for this to be real, for Logan to love her, to want to spend his life with her.

He ended the kiss and, after searching her face, started rowing again and Rebecca decided that sometimes it was best if they didn't speak. If she didn't let the feelings—insecurities and hopes—that she wasn't supposed to have bubble to the surface.

On the dock ahead of them a small group of photographers gathered. She sighed and Logan glanced back, scowling when he saw the pack. "Either we were followed or the boat owner must have called."

"My reputation," she said as pieces started to fall into place.

"What about it?"

"That was your other reason for getting engaged now. You wanted to protect my reputation after that photo of my car at your apartment."

He again looked back over his shoulder to the photographers. His face darkening.

"That's sweet. Thank you."

His strokes slowed. "This is supposed to be good for both of us. So far it seems to be working mostly in my favor."

"I don't know. It's doing what I need it to. And there have been other...benefits," she said, thinking, as she did far too often, of how they'd made love, knowing he'd know that was what she was thinking of. She'd hoped to make him smile with the reference. She didn't succeed.

They neared the dock.

"Once the news is released there will be questions." She pointed out the obvious.

"Like, when's the wedding going to be?"

She nodded.

"In ten months."

"You sound certain."

"I had to talk your father down from eighteen months. He insists that at least that much time is necessary to arrange a proper royal wedding. And after Rafe and Lexie snuck off for theirs and cheated him and the country of that celebration he is insisting on a proper royal wedding. But I wanted to be convincing, which meant I needed to stick as close to the truth as possible. If we really were getting married I'd want it to be as soon as feasible. I wouldn't want to waste another day not being married to you."

He would have had no difficulty convincing her father. He almost had her convinced—so badly was she blurring the lines between reality and fantasy.

Logan flicked another glance at the small group on the dock. "As for where we're going to live I don't see why we can't spend half the year here and half the year in the States. If your father and your adoring public would allow it. And if you wanted to."

"Sounds perfect." Almost too perfect. They may as well get their story straight.

"Babies?"

"Eventually," she answered, letting herself believe the

fantasy they were weaving. "We'll want some time together alone first."

"Long evenings when we can make love."

"And you can play the guitar for me."

"Definitely. And you can make us pancakes for breakfast."

"Definitely." She looked at her hand. The ring that represented so much and so little, sparkled.

Thirteen

The ring still sparkled but in the space of a day everything else had changed. Yesterday afternoon Rebecca had—for a blissful time—willfully indulged in the fantasy and allowed herself to be happy, even though it was all a pretence.

She didn't even have that now.

Now she was both executioner and victim.

Wearing a vibrant glittering red dress, a far cry from the somber mood that gripped her, she sat at Logan's side for the official dinner, her head swimming, her heart heavy.

As Eduardo had requested, she'd made time to speak with him. Just two hours ago.

And everything had changed.

She'd then spoken with her father. And her father had had to call in his aides to let them know of the changes in the dinner plans.

Usually these evenings dragged. But tonight the pre-dinner

socializing, and the dinner itself, sped by. She hadn't had a chance to be alone with Logan, who wore a tuxedo better than any man she'd ever met. And she'd wanted and needed that chance desperately, while at the same time hoping it would never come. She'd hoped to delay doing what she now had to do.

It wouldn't hurt him, she told herself. It wouldn't even hurt her. He'd get what he'd wanted and so would she. She was just speeding things up a little. So why did she feel so wretched?

Her father stood to make his after-dinner speech. Logan reached over and squeezed her hand, his thumb swept over her fingers. Frowning, he dropped his gaze to her bare left hand.

His beautiful ring was back in its box, making a small bulge in her evening bag.

"You're waiting for the official announcement?" He glanced at her father as the prince began speaking then back at her.

Rebecca bit her lip and shook her head. "There's a change of plan. Our engagement isn't being announced tonight."

Doubt clouded his eyes. They sat through the announcement of Lexie's pregnancy. She got the feeling it was as difficult for Logan, knowing something was wrong, as it was for her to join in the air of excitement and joy. Her father sat down to rapturous applause. Animated conversation erupted around the room.

Logan's gaze rested unnervingly on her. "Where can we go to talk?"

"I can't leave the dinner. Royal protocol." A protocol she was choosing to follow when, if she really wanted, she could arrange to slip out. But she couldn't be alone with Logan right now. She wasn't strong enough to do what she had to if he was questioning her, pressing for an explanation.

Music, an upbeat waltz, began to play. Couples filled the dance floor.

Logan sat stock-still at her side. "Is this about what I said the other morning?" His voice was a low whisper beneath the sound of the music. "About you not meaning anything to me. I thought we sorted that out. You know it wasn't true."

She could not let him believe that. Not now. "No," she said, "this is about me not wanting to go on with this charade." Her own words tore at her. She reached for her evening bag and felt inside for the small velvet box. Her hand closed around it and she clutched it for just a second before drawing the box out. Beneath the table, she slid it to Logan. His hands stayed clenched into fists on his thighs. She took a breath and called up the awful, gut-wrenching words she'd rehearsed as she'd dressed. "I don't want to pretend to be engaged to you."

Quite the contrary. She'd realized when she'd spoken to her father earlier, telling him not to announce their engagement, that what she wanted more than anything was to make what she had with Logan real.

That she loved him.

In an awful irony the lie she'd had to tell her father was not that she loved Logan when she didn't, but that she didn't love him when she did.

His hand closed around hers and the small box within it. "Put it back. I'm not taking it from you."

As Rebecca slipped the ring back into her bag, the man seated on her right leaned in to speak. Logan got in first. "Excuse us, please. We're about to dance."

He led her to the dance floor, pulled her in close to him with the hand that curved about her waist.

Dancing with him was effortless. He moved with such assured grace, his body in tune with hers. As she should have known he would be. As she'd never get to experience again. She gave herself a few stolen seconds, stored away the sensation. She could lean her head on his shoulder now, all too easily. Now when she wouldn't let herself. The seconds were exquisite torture.

"What's going on?" his low voice whispered in her ear.

She swallowed. She had to do this. She'd known that what they had would end. But not like this. Not by her own hand. And not so soon. She pulled back from him a little and smiled brightly, aware of the brittleness of her expression. "Nothing's going on. I realized I don't want to go through with this." She spoke dismissively. "That's all."

"This?"

"The charade of an engagement."

He leaned back enough to watch her face. "What's wrong?"

The concern in his gaze, a concern that was all for her, nearly undid her. He wasn't buying her indifference. And she knew he'd try to find a way to push and probe until he uncovered the truth of what was happening. If he knew she was doing this for him he wouldn't let her. That was how he was. He'd insist on honoring his side of the bargain. A bargain that felt more hollow than ever.

So she said the only thing she knew would make him back off. "I had time to think after we got back from the lake and I've realized there might be other men I'd like to date. Men from my own social milieu." She lifted her fingers from his shoulder and waved to an imaginary friend across the room. She swallowed again and lifted one suddenly cold shoulder in a shrug. "My father's list might not have been so terrible."

"That polo player?" he asked through gritted teeth.

Rebecca tried for a playful smile, as though she wasn't breaking her own heart, shattering her own dreams. "Amongst others. He wanted to take me to the opera next weekend. I thought that might be nice. And I know you don't like the opera."

"Nice?" Logan stopped dead, his jaw hard, a muscle working high up, near his ear. He studied her as though he'd never seen her before in his life. The music still played, dancers swirled around them. For a moment she thought he might walk away, leave her standing alone on the dance floor.

But his grip on her hand, and his hold at her waist, tightened. His gaze narrowed and darkened. "Will you come outside with me, somewhere where we can talk properly, and tell me what's really going on?"

"I can't leave the dinner," she said blithely, looking up at him. "It's just not done. And really, there's nothing I can add." She had to lock her knees to keep her legs from trembling.

"That's it?"

"It's for the best. No one was seriously going to believe we were a couple. I told my father not to announce our engagement because it was over between us. But it's been...fun. Thank you." She didn't know how she stood for so long smiling through his scrutiny. People moved around them, glancing curiously at them. Finally he lifted her hand and pressed his lips to her knuckles in the gentlest of kisses. A kiss that nearly undid her. Then he led her from the dance floor, dropped her hand and kept walking.

Rebecca didn't call out to him to ask—beg—him to come back, and she didn't run after him. Nor did she give in to the urge to flee and hide where she could lick her wounds, give in to the sobs that tried to force their way from her chest. She didn't do any of the things she wanted to do. She watched his back as he cut a swath through the milling guests, watched the top of his dark head until he was gone from her sight and then she returned to her seat and made polite conversation with the guests at the dinner. It was what she was trained to do.

Never had she needed her training more.

Two mornings later, Logan strode into the reception area of leBlanc Industries. This opportunity, he reminded himself as he looked around at the old world elegance, was all he'd wanted in establishing himself in this country. It was his entrée into the rest of Europe. The continuation of the expansion that had fueled his dreams for almost as long as he could remember.

Rebecca, who had left a gash in his heart, had been a means to that end. But not the only means. She'd been window dressing. He could do it without her.

He still didn't understand how he'd misjudged her and everything between them so badly. Still couldn't make sense of her sudden U-turn. Or his reaction to it. The loss of sleep that had nothing to do with a loss of business opportunities, or the bleakness of a day that held no promise of seeing her, hearing her voice, touching her.

He unclenched the hands at his side. He didn't need her. He'd bought in to or taken over numerous businesses in the past, all without her at his side. This would be no different. He looked to his future, a future with no place in it for a princess.

A personal assistant arrived to lead him to the boardroom. A dozen formally suited board members sat around the massive mahogany table, their smiles and body language receptive.

An hour later he strode out and boarded a plane for Chicago.

They'd offered him everything he wanted.

Fourteen

Rebecca fingered the thin gold chain around her neck as she skirted the crowded dance floor. All she really wanted was to escape the ball being held in her honor. The ball that had been intended to help her choose a suitor.

Tonight only Adam was fulfilling their father's expectations, dutifully dancing beneath the glittering chandeliers with almost every hopeful female attending, though none more than once.

Rebecca had danced with no one.

Because she had driven away the only man she wanted.

She had set herself the challenge of staying until midnight, but the minutes and hours had dragged. Soon though she would be able to leave. Alone. She had just one thing to do first.

Eduardo had been avoiding her since their last meeting.

The day Logan had walked out of her life and gone back to Chicago.

Eduardo's practiced smile dimmed and grew wary as she approached and unclenched her jaw enough to ask him to dance.

This was the only way to guarantee he would talk to her, to guarantee that she would keep a rein on her emotions and guarantee a specific end point to their conversation.

Their plan—hers and Logan's—had worked even when she'd wanted it not to. Despite her efforts to conceal her despair, her father had sensed its depths and offered to cancel the ball. He said he'd seen how upset she was over the end of her relationship with Logan. But she had insisted the ball go on. Because *upset* didn't even begin to describe her desolation.

That she'd done the right thing was little consolation.

When Logan had left she'd needed to rant and rave and so in the privacy of her bedroom those first nights she'd given vent to her heartbreak and grief and it had made her laugh and then cry harder to think that Logan would be proud of her for yielding to her emotions, for allowing herself to be overcome by them. As if she'd had a choice.

She walked to the dance floor with a tellingly silent Eduardo.

It was duty that had kept her going. She'd thrown herself back into work even as she'd felt like a hologram of herself. She had filled every hour of every day in a fruitless attempt to ensure she had no time to think about Logan, to dwell on him, to compare the emptiness of her life now to its fullness while he'd been in it. But no matter how busy she kept herself, thoughts of Logan underscored or overlaid every single thing she did. There was always time to think about him.

She dwelled.

Compounding her misery over the loss of him was the hurt of knowing how badly he must be thinking of her.

His good opinion mattered more than anyone else's in the world. And she had lost it. He believed she'd coldly reneged on their agreement and their relationship because she wanted to see other men.

As if any other man could compare.

She dwelled while she'd sat on boards, and attended openings. While she drove to kindergartens and hospitals. She dwelled when she fell into bed at night and couldn't sleep. She imagined him back in Chicago. Wondered what he was doing. Whether he thought of her.

And the pain and heartache had all been for nothing.

For which she blamed the man with whom she now danced, resenting every second of the touch of his hand to hers.

There was a wretched part of her that knew she should probably thank Eduardo. He had merely precipitated the inevitable and preordained conclusion. If her time with Logan had gone on longer, the trauma of the end, as overwhelming as it was, would have been even more devastating.

When she thought she had mastery over her voice and the storm of anger and grief within her, she spoke. "You broke our bargain." Her voice was gratifyingly steady. "I never thought you'd stoop so low." She wasn't yet ready to thank him. "You couldn't seriously think I would ever go out with you again, no matter how well that would reflect on you or how much political capital your stepfather would gain from the association."

Eduardo frowned and stiffened. "I kept our bargain."

Rebecca gave an unprincesslike snort of derision. "Our bargain was that Logan got the approval he needed if we weren't together."

"He had the board's approval. He turned it down."

"*He* turned it down? I don't believe you. It was everything he wanted."

"He turned it down flat and walked out of the meeting. And don't look at me like that. It was nothing to do with me. The board members were as perplexed as you."

"But…"

Eduardo moved and spoke stiffly. "Whatever happened, and for whatever reason, I still say no good—for you or the country—could have come from a relationship between you and Logan Buchanan. He was wrong for you. Utterly wrong. In time you'll see that."

"I doubt it."

"Then you're not the woman I thought you were."

She disengaged her hand from his and stepped away. "I've never been the woman you thought I was." The only man who'd ever seen the woman she really was had gone. She turned and walked back to her seat.

Midnight was only minutes away. Then she could leave and seek the sanctuary of her quiet, dark, Logan-less room.

She tried her best to be attentive to her table companions, to play her part.

A couple of times she caught Adam, in the arms of one or another beautiful woman, frowning at her. He would have to do his royal duty for the both of them. It didn't look as though it was too much of a hardship for him.

Finally, finally she heard the slow distant chime of the tower clock. As politely as she could—hiding her desire to flee—she excused herself.

She made it outside, to the top of the broad sweeping stairs, and closed her eyes on the welling tears. She drew in a deep, shuddering breath just as the twelfth chime of midnight sounded on the air. Her fingers sought the chain about her neck. And despite knowing better, despite the futility, she couldn't help but wish that she could wind back the clock and do everything differently. That she could have one more chance with Logan.

She'd never told him she loved him. The love that in a different lifetime would have been a joy was now her burden.

Footsteps approached. She waited for them to pass. She needed just a moment before she faced her life again...

"You're going about this all wrong." A deep, low voice sounded by her ear. And even though she tried to tamp down the vicious flare of hope, because Logan had gone back to his life in Chicago, she whirled to face the speaker. Daring to hope.

And her heart soared.

Logan searched her face, just as she drank in the angry, beautiful sight of him, as though it had been an eternity, not a handful of days since she'd last seen him. She catalogued and savored his features, the hard line of his jaw, the tense set to his shoulders and the smoldering depths of his eyes. And the roughness to his breath, as though he'd just sprinted the dozens of stairs. His bow tie dangled undone about his neck. His presence, so longed for, felt almost like an apparition, like the unexpected granting of her deepest wish. So surreal that she feared at any moment he might vanish.

She longed to reach for him, to touch his face, to throw her arms around him. But the foreboding in his gaze held her still. "I thought you were in Chicago."

"I was. I had commitments there."

"But you've come back?"

"Because I have commitments here, too." He lifted his hands to her face and she saw in his eyes, and in the dark shadows beneath them, something of her own torment. His gaze dipped to the chain around her neck.

"If you want to get rid of me," he said, "the very last

thing you should tell me is that I'm second choice. It just makes me determined to win."

No words came as he watched her, waited for her response. "That was what you were trying to do, wasn't it? To get rid of me?"

And despite the fact that the denial and explanation stayed trapped in her throat, he lowered his hands and looped his arms around her waist to pull her close. As though he craved the connection of touch as desperately as she did.

She ought to pull back.

Instead she clung. She took pleasure in his nearness and his touch, in his scent and his warmth. She closed her eyes and breathed deeply, trying to inhale the very essence of him.

In spite of the tension vibrating from him she dared to hope.

He had come back.

To the music that drifted from within the great hall, he began swaying with her. He edged them away from the wide doors, away from the guests coming and leaving.

The voice of doubt and self-preservation wouldn't give up. She couldn't jump to conclusions just because this was what she ached for. He'd come back, but why and for how long? "You didn't buy the subsidiary."

"No." He held her tighter.

"But it was everything you wanted. Everything you'd worked toward."

He stopped moving. "*It* wasn't everything I wanted. I don't take well to being manipulated. And I don't need your charity."

She pulled back at the accusation in his tone. He loosened his hold only enough that she could see his face. "Manipulated? Charity?"

"I won board approval only after I told them our relationship had ended. They were prepared to award it *because* you and I were no longer an item. And the man behind it all, the one looking the smuggest, was your old friend's new stepfather."

Rebecca gasped. "You didn't take it because of pride? You threw away everything you'd worked toward because you were miffed?"

"No."

"Then, why?" The words hiccupped in her throat, caught behind a sob. So much pain and for what?

"Because I needed to prove something."

"Point scoring? With Eduardo and his stepfather?"

"No. With you."

"I don't understand." Her anger was beginning to rival the one she sensed in him.

"Answer this. Why did you send me away?"

"I wanted to give you what you wanted. Eduardo guaranteed you would win the bid, but only if we were no longer together. I did you a favor."

"And you didn't trust me enough to tell me what your so-called friend had said, let me find a way around it?"

"I knew you'd think you had to honor your side of the bargain and give me the public engagement we'd agreed on. But it would cost you what you wanted. You could at least appreciate the sacrifice."

He stilled. "So it was a sacrifice? Ending what we had?"

He lifted both hands to her jaw, tilting her head up, forcing her to meet his gaze.

"Yes. But it was the right thing to do. And I'd do the same again. We were ending anyway."

"Were we?"

"That's what we'd agreed." That simple agreement seemed like a lifetime ago.

"Yes. It was," he said gently. "But when the end came, it turned out to be not at all what I expected. Or wanted."

"That's why you didn't buy into leBlanc? It doesn't make sense."

Something softened in his gaze. He lowered his hands to loop them behind her back again and began moving slowly with her, not waltzing, just swaying. Together. "Nothing about us makes sense on the surface. But here," he brushed his fingers over his heart, shifted them to where hers pounded with hope, "here it makes sense." Then he scooped a finger beneath the chain that hung around her neck, dipping below the neckline of her dress. Lifting the chain, he pulled up its secret treasure. The ring that hung hidden against her chest. She couldn't wear it on her finger but she had wanted it close, wanted to wear it somehow.

"You're wearing my ring."

There was no response she could give that wouldn't incriminate her. She'd tried but hadn't been able to give up the ring, had needed to keep it close. So she opted for full-on incrimination and whispered, "Always."

"The reason I didn't take the opportunity you so nobly offered was because I needed you to know that when I came to you to tell you I love you and ask you to marry me, that I was doing it for you alone. *You* are everything I want."

Logan reached behind her neck and undid the clasp of her chain then removed the necklace and let the ring slide into his upturned palm. He picked up her hand and, holding her gaze, his eyes seeking permission, he waited for her nod before sliding the ring onto her finger.

"I want you, Rebecca Marconi. I want you in every possible sense of the word. Forever. I love you and I want you to share my life and I want to share yours. Whatever

I have to do to make that happen, whatever sacrifices and compromises are necessary will be worth it. Because nothing is as important to me as being with you." He paused for breath. "Will you marry me?"

Rebecca nodded as tears welled in her eyes. "Yes," she whispered. "Because I love you, too."

And then, finally, he kissed her.

Epilogue

Rebecca sat on the balcony and watched as the sun rose above the sea, turning the ocean golden, seeming for a moment to light it on fire. At a slight sound, she turned to watch Logan stroll out carrying two steaming mugs. He handed one to her before pulling a second chair close to hers and sitting down, resting his arm along the back of her seat.

"You were right about coming here."

"I knew you'd admit it eventually," he said with a wink.

Because he knew her too well. When he'd suggested coming back to New Zealand for a break, she'd argued against it. Their wedding was only two months away and the preparations were gaining pace, almost frenetically so. But that, he'd said, was precisely why she needed the break. Despite the occasional unnecessary panic by a staff member, everything was under control back home. Her schedule had been rearranged. She could be spared for a week. All the major decisions had been made long ago and the small ones could be dealt with by other people, or when they got back. And leaving the rain drenched fall back home for a crisp, sunny spring was a bonus, too. The hillside behind them rang with a chorus of birdsong.

Rebecca looked back out at the sunrise and breathed deeply. "Everything's so beautiful," she whispered, awe-struck. "So perfect."

"Especially you," he answered, sounding just as amazed. She turned to see him studying her. She never got tired of the way he looked at her, and her body never ceased to respond—whether they were alone like this, or in the midst of a crowded room at a royal function. She lit up for him like the ocean had for the sun. And he knew, and used shamelessly, the effect he had on her.

But the balance of power wasn't all in his favor. She had the same effect on him. She'd been able on more than one occasion to distract him from what he'd claimed was pressing business. She delighted in that power.

Today he wore faded jeans and a dark T-shirt, the same as he'd worn that first morning they'd both been on this same deck of Colleen's B & B. So male, so appealing. Despite how good he looked in a tuxedo, the jeans and T-shirt combination was her favorite. Other than when she stripped that T-shirt, and then the jeans, off him.

"Come and sit here." Logan patted his lap and grinned. She went to him—she always did—and sat, reveling in the feel of his broad chest behind her and his powerful thighs beneath her. He wrapped his arms around her, held her to him. "Have I told you I love you, today?"

"Yes." And she had told him the same.

She leaned back against his chest. "You're sure I'm not too heavy for you?"

Behind her, she felt him shake his head and then press a kiss to the side of her neck. "Never."

"Never?"

"Never." He kissed her again.

"What if I was pregnant? I don't think I'd fit."

"You'll always fit. There will always be room for you." She heard the hint of curiosity in his voice, and the arms that had held her tight shifted. He moved his hands till they rested over her abdomen, still flat beneath her jeans. "Especially when you're pregnant."

They'd been planning on having children soon after they were married and had been careful. But there had been occasions when enthusiasm overrode care.

His hands shifted again, and he lifted and turned her so that she sat sideways across his lap rather than with her back to his chest. "Are you trying to tell me something?"

She nodded. "I saw my doctor yesterday."

Logan's jaw dropped and myriad emotions flitted through his eyes and across his face. For the first time since they'd known each other, she saw a hint of tears in his beautiful eyes.

He placed a hand over her stomach again, gentle yet possessive. "When?"

"Just over eight months. It's very early yet. Too early to tell anyone else. Especially because the first trimester is the most tenuous."

"The flight?" he said, a note of panic in his voice.

"Pregnant women fly all the time. It's fine." She slipped her arms around his neck, loving how this man, so confident in every aspect of his life, looked suddenly uncertain. But gradually that uncertainty faded from his face and was replaced by joy and pride.

"I won't even be showing in my wedding dress. But people will be able to do the math once he or she is born."

"Who cares?"

"You don't mind that it's so soon?"

"Mind? After your 'I love you' and your 'yes' to my proposal, that's the most wonderful thing I've ever heard you say." His eyes drifted closed as he held her to him, one hand still on her stomach as though trying to sense the life they'd created growing there.

He opened his eyes. "How will your father take it? The timing?"

"Initially he'll be a little put out. He does like things to be done 'properly.' But hard on the heels of that reaction will be joy at another grandchild. What with Bonnie already with a stranglehold over his heart he won't stand a chance." Rafe and Lexie's little girl was the light of her father's life. Time and again she'd watched her father turn from being a reigning monarch to a sappy, doting grandfather the moment he set eyes on Bonnie. "All it needs for Dad's world to be complete is for Adam to find someone he loves."

"How's Adam going with that?"

"He's giving it his best shot. Doing everything he ought. But…I don't know. Adam's always been too academic about things, thinking he can analyze and then control how life ought to unfold. I'm worried he'll pick someone because she meets a list of criteria he's drawn up for himself rather than someone who gets beneath his skin and into his heart even though on paper she might not be right for him."

"Like you did to me," he said. His hand shifted from her stomach to her thigh.

"And you to me."

"Adam's a smart man. He'll figure it out."

"Not so smart about everything."

"He'll figure it out. Besides, he's got Rafe and Lexie and now us showing him how it ought to be done."

"Maybe you're right."

"You know I am. But I didn't bring you here to talk about your brother." His hand curved around her thigh. "Do you remember the first time I saw you in jeans?"

How could she forget? They'd made love that night for the first time. "Yes." She brushed a kiss across his lips.

He reached for her head, brought it close again so that he could return the kiss, deepening it.

He pulled back and she looked into his beautiful eyes, watched his lips curve into the smile she loved so much. With one mind they stood. Leaving the sunrise, and their drinks on the table, they headed back inside.

* * * * *

COMING NEXT MONTH

Available August 9, 2011

#2101 MARRIAGE AT THE COWBOY'S COMMAND
Ann Major

#2102 THE REBEL TYCOON RETURNS
Katherine Garbera
Texas Cattleman's Club: The Showdown

#2103 TO TOUCH A SHEIKH
Olivia Gates
Pride of Zohayd

#2104 HOW TO SEDUCE A BILLIONAIRE
Kate Carlisle

#2105 CLAIMING HIS ROYAL HEIR
Jennifer Lewis
Billionaires and Babies

#2106 A CLANDESTINE CORPORATE AFFAIR
Michelle Celmer
Black Gold Billionaires

HDCNM0711

REQUEST YOUR FREE BOOKS!

2 FREE NOVELS PLUS 2 FREE GIFTS!

Harlequin®

Desire

ALWAYS POWERFUL, PASSIONATE AND PROVOCATIVE

YES! Please send me 2 FREE Harlequin Desire® novels and my 2 FREE gifts (gifts are worth about $10). After receiving them, if I don't wish to receive any more books, I can return the shipping statement marked "cancel." If I don't cancel, I will receive 6 brand-new novels every month and be billed just $4.30 per book in the U.S. or $4.99 per book in Canada. That's a saving of at least 14% off the cover price! It's quite a bargain! Shipping and handling is just 50¢ per book in the U.S. and 75¢ per book in Canada.* I understand that accepting the 2 free books and gifts places me under no obligation to buy anything. I can always return a shipment and cancel at any time. Even if I never buy another book, the two free books and gifts are mine to keep forever.

225/326 HDN FEF3

Name	(PLEASE PRINT)

Address		Apt. #

City	State/Prov.	Zip/Postal Code

Signature (if under 18, a parent or guardian must sign)

Mail to the **Reader Service:**
IN U.S.A.: P.O. Box 1867, Buffalo, NY 14240-1867
IN CANADA: P.O. Box 609, Fort Erie, Ontario L2A 5X3

Not valid for current subscribers to Harlequin Desire books.

Want to try two free books from another line?
Call 1-800-873-8635 or visit www.ReaderService.com.

* Terms and prices subject to change without notice. Prices do not include applicable taxes. Sales tax applicable in N.Y. Canadian residents will be charged applicable taxes. Offer not valid in Quebec. This offer is limited to one order per household. All orders subject to credit approval. Credit or debit balances in a customer's account(s) may be offset by any other outstanding balance owed by or to the customer. Please allow 4 to 6 weeks for delivery. Offer available while quantities last.

Your Privacy—The Reader Service is committed to protecting your privacy. Our Privacy Policy is available online at www.ReaderService.com or upon request from the Reader Service.

We make a portion of our mailing list available to reputable third parties that offer products we believe may interest you. If you prefer that we not exchange your name with third parties, or if you wish to clarify or modify your communication preferences, please visit us at www.ReaderService.com/consumerchoice or write to us at Reader Service Preference Service, P.O. Box 9062, Buffalo, NY 14269. Include your complete name and address.

HDES11B

*Once bitten, twice shy. That's Gabby Wade's motto—
especially when it comes to Adamson men.
And the moment she meets Jon Adamson her theory
is confirmed. But with each encounter a little something
sparks between them, making her wonder if she's been
too hasty to dismiss this one!*

*Enjoy this sneak peek from ONE GOOD REASON
by Sarah Mayberry, available August 2011
from Harlequin® Superromance®.*

Gabby Wade's heartbeat thumped in her ears as she marched to her office. She wanted to pretend it was because of her brisk pace returning from the file room, but she wasn't that good a liar.

Her heart was beating like a tom-tom because Jon Adamson had touched her. In a very male, very possessive way. She could still feel the heat of his big hand burning through the seat of her khakis as he'd steadied her on the ladder.

It had taken every ounce of self-control to tell him to unhand her. What she'd really wanted was to grab him by his shirt and, well, explore all those urges his touch had instantly brought to life.

While she might not like him, she was wise enough to understand that it wasn't always about liking the other person. Sometimes it was about pure animal attraction.

Refusing to think about it, she turned to work. When she'd typed in the wrong figures three times, Gabby admitted she was too tired and too distracted. Time to call it a day.

As she was leaving, she spied Jon at his workbench in the shop. His head was propped on his hand as he studied blueprints. It wasn't until she got closer that she saw his eyes were shut.

He looked oddly boyish. There was something innocent and unguarded in his expression. She felt a weakening in her resistance to him.

"Jon." She put her hand on his shoulder, intending to shake him awake. Instead, it rested there like a caress.

His eyes snapped open.

"You were asleep."

"No, I was, uh, visualizing something on this design." He gestured to the blueprint in front of him then rubbed his eyes.

That gesture dealt a bigger blow to her resistance. She realized it wasn't only animal attraction pulling them together. She took a step backward as if to get away from the knowledge.

She cleared her throat. "I'm heading off now."

He gave her a smile, and she could see his exhaustion.

"Yeah, I should, too." He stood and stretched. The hem of his T-shirt rose as he arched his back and she caught a flash of hard male belly. She looked away, but it was too late. Her mind had committed the image to permanent memory.

And suddenly she knew, for good or bad, she'd never look at Jon the same way again.

Find out what happens next in ONE GOOD REASON, available August 2011 from Harlequin® Superromance®!

Celebrating

Blaze **10** *years of* **red-hot reads**

Featuring a special August author lineup of
six fan-favorite authors who have written
for Blaze™ from the beginning!

The Original Sexy Six:

Vicki Lewis Thompson
Tori Carrington
Kimberly Raye
Debbi Rawlins
Julie Leto
Jo Leigh

Pick up all six Blaze™
Special Collectors' Edition titles!

August 2011

HBCELEBRATE0811